SKY JUMPERS

PEGGY EDDLEMAN

A Yearling Book

Text copyright © 2013 by Peggy Eddleman
Cover art copyright © 2013 by Owen Richardson
Map art copyright © 2013 by Jeff Nentrup

All rights reserved. Published in the United States by Yearling, an imprint of Random House Children's Books, a division of Random House LLC, a Penguin Random House Company, New York. Originally published in hardcover in the United States by Random House Children's Books, New York, in 2013.

Yearling and the jumping horse design are registered trademarks of Random House LLC.

Visit us on the Web! randomhouse.com/kids

Educators and librarians, for a variety of teaching tools, visit us at RHTeachersLibrarians.com

The Library of Congress has cataloged the hardcover edition of this work as follows:
Eddleman, Peggy.
Sky jumpers / by Peggy Eddleman. — 1st ed.
p. cm.
Summary: "Twelve-year-old Hope lives in a post–World War III town called White Rock where everyone must participate in Inventions Day, though Hope's inventions always fail. Her unique skill set comes in handy when a group of bandits invades the town."
—Provided by publisher.
ISBN 978-0-307-98127-1 (trade) — ISBN 978-0-307-98128-8 (lib. bdg.) —
ISBN 978-0-307-98129-5 (ebook)
[1. Inventions—Fiction. 2. Science fiction.] I. Title.
PZ7.E2129Th 2013 [Fic]—dc23 2012027037

ISBN 978-0-307-98130-1 (pbk.)

Printed in the United States of America

10 9 8 7 6 5 4 3

First Yearling Edition 2014

For Lance
Who has believed in me, supported me,
and cheered me on, every step of the way

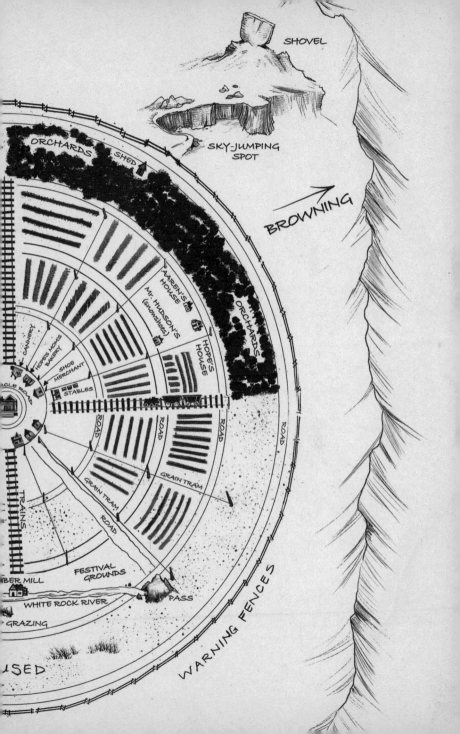

The Bomb's Breath

You would think I'd never jumped off a cliff before, based on how long I stood there. Not jumping.

Of course, I'd never made *this* jump before.

Aaren and I hadn't been up here for two weeks, and I missed this place. We came today as my reward for finally finishing my invention. It was going to show everyone that for the first time since I was born twelve years ago, I wasn't the worst in town at inventing. I was even sure there was no way for this one to hurt anyone or do any damage.

When a gust of wind hit from behind and blew my hair out of my ponytail and into my face, I breathed in the fall air the morning sun had just begun to warm. Every part of my body tingled with excitement thinking about the jump Brock had challenged me to make. I stood at the edge of the cliff looking across the area where I knew the invisible Bomb's Breath spread across our valley, wishing Brock had shown up to watch me jump like he'd said he would.

But I needed to stop thinking about him and focus. Aaren and his five-year-old sister, Brenna, looked up at me with encouraging faces from the rock ledge I planned to land on just over thirty-five feet below. I made note of the wiry bush that grew out of a crack in the cliff face and told me where the Bomb's Breath began. The fact that the Bomb's Breath was invisible was one of the most dangerous things about it.

The fact that it would kill you if you took even one breath in it was the other dangerous part, but the Bomb's Breath was still my favorite side effect left behind by the green bombs of World War III. Mr. Hudson, our inventions teacher in Tens & Elevens, said that the way the oxygen molecules got cross-linked and bonded together made the air feel much denser than the regular air above and below the fifteen-foot-thick band. You couldn't breathe in the oxygen molecules separately and your body couldn't absorb them together, so you'd suffocate instantly if you inhaled while in the midst of the Bomb's Breath.

It was Aaren who came up with the theory that we could hold our breath and walk into it. Based on the horrified look on his face when I first tested his theory, he'd have never told me if he'd known I'd try it. But I had trusted Aaren's theories ever since we were five, and he told me that I could grab on to a skinny branch of the willow tree I was stuck in and it would lower me to the ground slowly enough. His theories were never wrong, so of course I'd try out his Bomb's Breath theory.

It took my walking into it twice, and nonstop talking about how incredible it was to be in air that *felt* so much thicker but *looked* the same, before he and his scientific brain had to test it, too. It was me, though, who figured out we could sky jump into the Bomb's Breath and it would slow our fall. Like we had wings.

After I jumped off this cliff, I'd have about fifteen feet of regular air to do a double front flip before I hit the air of the Bomb's Breath. My head would be the last thing to right itself, so I wouldn't be able to see the bush growing from the crack. And that meant I wouldn't be able to see when I needed to take my last breath.

I pulled my necklace from behind my shirt and rubbed my thumb over the rough stone. Not for luck, and definitely not because I was scared. I rubbed it because it was the only object in existence left by my birth mom before I was adopted. I didn't know her before she died, but I knew she was brave. Whenever I touched the coarse, uneven surface, I was reminded that she did impossible things, and so could I.

"Hope!" Aaren yelled up to me. His sand-colored curly

hair glinted in the morning sun. "Just because Brock said you can't make the jump doesn't mean you have to try. If you can't make it, you can come down."

I laughed, because egging someone on was something I did, not him. Aaren and I had been friends for twelve years—since we were newborn babies and our moms put us in the same crib for naps—so he knew if someone told me I couldn't do something, I'd do it just to prove them wrong. This was Aaren's way of saying he knew I could do it and to hurry up about it.

I agreed. I pushed the necklace inside my shirt, then jumped into the sky.

Air rushed past as I threw my arms forward and tucked into a ball, the long hair of my ponytail flapping in the wind. The first front flip was easy—I'd landed that one a dozen times from the cliff that sat barely above the Bomb's Breath. It was the second one that made me nervous, so I sucked in the hugest breath I could manage before I rotated into it, even though I should have waited a little longer to take that last breath. As my view changed from the bushes below to the cliff, I tucked harder, hoping for more momentum. When the cliff gave way to sky, I straightened my body just as I plunged into the air of the Bomb's Breath.

This was, without a doubt, my favorite part.

The Bomb's Breath slowed my fall as I sank to the middle

of the band of pressurized air. I stretched my arms and legs out and imagined I was held in midair by invisible hands as I slowly floated downward, feeling utterly and completely free. Sometimes I kicked my feet and windmilled my arms like I was swimming in the lake. If I kicked hard enough, I could stay in it a little longer. But taking that breath so early made my lungs burn. As much as I wanted to play around, I needed to get out so I could take a breath. Soon.

I squirmed until I managed to get into an upright position. The Bomb's Breath ended about six feet above the rock ledge, so I kicked my feet back and forth as I drifted down toward it, feeling the drag of the heavy air with every kick. When my feet swung without any resistance, I braced myself as gravity pulled me more than the Bomb's Breath held me. I dropped out of the Bomb's Breath and landed on the rocky ledge in a crouch, then gasped for air.

The excitement of the jump filled my chest with a crazy humming, like dozens of miniature birds lifting me off the ground. "I did it! A double front flip!" I wanted to shout it to the world. Of course, Brock was the only person I could tell who wasn't already standing with me. I wished he'd seen me. I shook off the regret and smiled—at least I knew I would *really* enjoy telling him.

Aaren looked as happy as I felt and gave me a "good job" nod. Brenna planted a running hug on me. Even though she was only five years old and small, it would've knocked me down if I hadn't been expecting it. With Brenna, though, I always expected it.

"I knew you could do it," she said. "Aaren told me you could and I knew you could but you took so long. I thought maybe you were too scared, but Aaren told me that you weren't scared, you just didn't know it yet, and to be patient because you *could* do it. And you did! You jumped and you did the flips!"

I scoffed in Aaren's direction. "I wasn't scared."

"Then what took so long? Admiring the scenery?"

I looked up at the ledge I'd stood on moments before, which now seemed so teeny. "Nah. I was just enjoying how fresh the air smelled when I wasn't standing right next to you." I winked at Brenna to make sure she knew I was just teasing her brother.

Okay, so maybe it wasn't the best choice in comebacks. Aaren's family and mine were farm partners, so I knew for a fact that he'd weeded his family's personal garden before we left, and he'd probably bathed right after. I, on the other hand, had cleaned out the chicken coops. Nastiest job on our farm. The whole time I worked, I thought about how much I wanted to get in a few celebratory jumps before school. And how much I wanted to prove to Brock that I could do a double flip. In my rush to get to the mountain, I didn't even bathe. I probably still smelled like a chicken coop. But that wasn't the most important thing.

"What do you think Brock's going to say when I tell him I made it?"

"Nothing," Aaren said.

"Yeah." I sighed. "You're probably right. You know, we should tell him that when you challenge someone and they win, it's only polite to say how upset you are about it. Possibly even yell. Stomp your feet. *Something*."

"The world would be a better place if everyone knew that," Aaren joked.

"Wouldn't it?" I grabbed Brenna's hand to leave, then I stepped so my body was between her and the dead squirrel I'd just noticed a few feet up the mountain. We saw a dead animal right at the edge of the Bomb's Breath almost every time, but I was determined to keep Brenna from seeing them. She knew how dangerous it was even without the reminder. Everyone did. It was one of the first things we learned as little kids. The fences were really only there to keep the cows and sheep away. The people of White Rock didn't dare come anywhere near the Bomb's Breath.

With each step down the mountain, it felt like I floated more than walked. I could've lived off the thrill from that double flip for days. Even if no one else knew outside of Brock, Aaren, and Brenna, doing tricks into the Bomb's Breath was what made me special. Different. It was one thing I was really good at.

I moved aside some branches from a bush and led Brenna through the mostly nonexistent path.

"When are you gonna let *me* go sky jumping?" Brenna asked, just like every time we brought her up here.

Aaren gave his usual answer. "Not until you're ten, like we were."

And maybe not even then, I thought. A lot of smart people lived in my town, and they all stayed far away from the Bomb's Breath.

I was still holding Brenna's hand as the three of us got to the part where several boulders lay together, making the ground drop three feet. Aaren climbed down first. I lowered Brenna to him, then climbed down myself. The rest of the way wasn't as rough, so we ran.

We stopped to catch our breath just before the warning fences. This was the best view of our perfectly round valley, ten miles in diameter and ringed by mountains. Across the valley, White Rock River cut through the mountain, making the passageway that provided the only route into White Rock. Our valley was actually a huge crater left behind by the green bomb that hit the plains of Cook, Nebraska, forty years ago. We weren't near the top of the crater by a long shot—it actually went up for miles past where I jumped.

I smiled as I looked across at the homes and farms set in rings all the way down to City Circle at the bottom.

Even if all the people in town weren't deathly afraid of the Bomb's Breath, I was still probably the only one who could've landed that jump. Well, except for possibly Brock.

People always said that the Bomb's Breath covered the entire Earth, but most people didn't have it close enough to worry about or to play in like we did. I guess that wasn't a bad thing. People were more afraid of the Bomb's Breath than they were of the bandits who roamed the plains, even though the bandits were attacking more and more. But at least in White Rock we were safe. Completely protected. And as long as Aaren and I didn't get caught, we could sneak off to sky jump.

We yanked our schoolbags from where we'd hidden them under a chokeberry bush on our way up. I ducked my head under my schoolbag strap and swung it onto my back so it wouldn't be in the way as I carefully picked up my invention. Today we were going to present our projects for the Harvest Festival. Inventions Day had been disastrous for me since we started school at age four. But this year was different. Just like every year, I had cuts and scrapes all over my arms and I still didn't get along with the equipment, but this year, everyone would be impressed with my invention.

Brenna grinned as she picked up hers. It was simple—a metal pot with a wide wooden spoon inside. She'd drilled holes in the spoon, so when she was mixing runny stuff for her mom, it would stir easier and get mixed better.

Aaren hadn't shown me his invention yet, but he'd already told me he'd found a way to make a thermometer so he could boil chemicals to an exact temperature to make medicines. The way he was headed, his split job would be the town doctor, just like his mom. He stuck his covered invention under the arm farthest from me like it was nothing. He probably held another festival-winning invention and didn't want me to feel bad that it was so easy for him.

I put one leg over the two horizontal logs nailed to posts that formed the warning fences, while imagining the look on my teacher's and Mr. Hudson's faces when they saw how much better I did this year.

I swung my second leg over, careful not to bump my invention, and my shorts caught on a splintery part of the top log. I didn't notice, so when I slid off, it tore a three-inch gash in the fabric near my knee. I couldn't go to school with torn shorts! My mind was running through possibilities for changing into pants that weren't ripped or finding a way to make it not noticeable, when the huge steam whistle at City Circle blew and jerked my thoughts away.

"It can't be time for the nine o'clock train already!" I looked to Aaren and Brenna, hoping I'd see reassurance, but instead I saw panic. Only for a second, though, because then they took off running.

Late

As much as I tried to hold my invention steady, it jostled as we sprinted through the orchard. I was torn between slowing down to keep my invention safe and speeding up to catch the train. A small part of me knew, though, that running faster wouldn't make a difference. "It's at least a mile and a half away," I panted. "We'll never make it that far in five minutes!"

Aaren ran faster. "We have to! My mom thought we took the eight o'clock train. If the school tells her we were late, she'll know we went somewhere else instead!"

If she knew where we'd been, things would get awful for all of us. I looked to Brenna as we ran. "You won't tell her where we were, right?"

She shook her head.

"She won't tell," Aaren said between huffs. "She's just not a good liar. My mom will be furious! We *have* to make it."

I'd gotten myself into trouble for plenty of things, but I'd never done anything else as bad as going into the Bomb's Breath. The people of White Rock had learned how deadly the Bomb's Breath was when one of the original settlers walked into it shortly after they started living here. The warning fences weren't built right away, though, because there were so many other things they had to build first. Everyone just knew to stay far from it. When my dad was seven years old, he and a dozen kids about his age were playing in the woods. They gradually moved closer and closer to the Bomb's Breath without even realizing it. During a game of tag, four kids ran right into the Bomb's Breath and died. Everyone in White Rock had a connection to at least one of them, so I understood why they were so terrified of the Bomb's Breath. I especially understood why my dad was—one of the four kids who'd died was his best friend. Things would be bad for me if I got caught.

But I'd still be better off than Aaren if his parents found out.

Aaren's mom had been with my dad when the kids died. Every parent felt an insanely huge responsibility to repopulate this near-empty world, and Aaren's were no exception. They had ten kids, and everything about Aaren's house and family was organized. The five oldest kids each had a younger sibling they looked out for, made sure got places, saw to the needs of, and most of all protected. Aaren would be in massive amounts of trouble for going beyond the fences, but it would be worse because they'd know he took Brenna there as well.

On his own, Aaren stayed far from trouble. With me, he always got into it. I liked to think he did crazy things with me because he had more fun around me. Knowing Aaren, though, it was probably because he wanted to make sure I stayed safe. Or that he was there to help me if I got injured. Letting him get caught for this wasn't an option. I managed to take a hand off my invention, grab Aaren's shoulder, and pull us both to a stop. "We have to find another way."

Aaren stopped running. "*What* other way? It's two miles from here to City Circle! With Brenna and our inventions, we won't make it until history's half over." He swung around like a trapped animal looking for escape. "We're going to be in so much trouble!"

I couldn't see anything past the trees, so my mind went to everything that lay beyond them. "Oh! The grain tram at the end of the orchard!"

"Neither of us is old enough *or* certified to use it," Aaren said.

"I've run the foot pedals with my dad since I was five. You know I can do it!"

He had that look on his face. The one where thoughts of getting into possibly more trouble battled with thoughts of escaping trouble. A little pang of guilt hit, thinking about how often I'd seen that face, and how often it had been because of me.

I bent down to Brenna's height. "Brenna, have you ever ridden on the grain tram?"

"No."

"Betcha always wanted to, though, right?"

Her eyes lit up and she turned to her brother. "Can we *please,* Aaren?"

I knew I had him. I swear, that girl was heaven-sent— Aaren's parents couldn't have paired him with a better sibling. Brenna idolized Aaren, and Aaren would do anything for her. This wasn't the first time I'd talked him into doing something crazy because of Brenna. But this time the crazy might actually keep him *out* of trouble.

The steam whistle blew twice, signaling the four trains at the top of their tracks in the north, south, east, and west to leave for City Circle. It was now official that we wouldn't make it.

Aaren glanced at Brenna, then at me. "Okay. We'll take the grain tram."

Brenna jumped up and down and cheered. I exhaled in relief. There was still a possibility I could save us.

It took ten minutes to run to the massive post that held the tram rope—long enough that the trains were probably close to City Circle, if they weren't there already. We pulled the rope to bring the square platform of the tram up to us from where it rested at the next farm down. Every invention used in White Rock had a plaque on it that gave credit to the person who invented it. As the tram neared, the sun caught the piece of flat metal nailed to its side, sparkling with David Romanek's name. He won the Harvest Festival Inventions Contest with it twenty years ago as a way for everyone to carry their grains and produce down to City Circle. Now twelve trams were in use throughout White Rock.

The six-foot-square platform had short walls on the front and on both sides. It hung from ropes on a pulley, so it hovered two feet above the ground. The pulley traveled on a thick rope that ran from the post at the top of the fourth ring all the way down to the post at City Circle. I sat at the brakes, and Aaren helped Brenna to a corner. He arranged the inventions so they wouldn't fall off, then he sat down. I released the stopper, and gravity pulled us down the hill.

The trick to the tram was to use the brakes to slow

it at key places. Otherwise, you'd barrel toward the town center, unable to stop because of the weight of the load. My dad had told me that after several people crashed their platform of goods through the post at the bottom of the line, they required people to certify on it. Even though I hadn't exactly driven it by myself before, I was sure I could be certified. It was entirely stupid that they didn't let twelve-year-olds take the test.

The tram rocked side to side from our speed, and an excited energy filled my stomach. Aaren grasped Brenna's shoulder as if she was going to fly away, but it wasn't like I was being unsafe. We *had* to hurry.

I pushed back the hair that had fallen out of my ponytail so I could see toward City Circle better, hoping to catch a glimpse of the train. It wasn't big enough to see over everyone's trees, though.

Since everything in the valley sloped upward, we used steam plows to flatten the land in sections, or rings. It looked like steps led up in all directions from City Circle. Well, steps if you were a giant with half-mile-long feet. The tram path, though, wasn't cut into steps; it just angled straight down. We whizzed past the freshly plowed fields of the third ring—the ring of farms that included my house.

"Hope!" Aaren screamed as the rocking almost knocked us into one of the support pillars at the end of the third ring.

I nodded and pushed on the stopper a bit, but went as fast through the second ring of farms as I dared. If anyone was working in their fields, I figured they'd have less of a chance to see us if we went so fast we were a blur. *Keep Aaren and Brenna out of trouble, and keep my invention safe.* That was all that really mattered.

Okay, so maybe my stop could've been a little smoother. But at least I got us near some bushes at the edge of the Kearneys' property, still far enough from the end that anyone in City Circle wouldn't see us get off. Aaren looked pale and was a bit unsteady as he climbed out of the tram, but I could tell he was grateful I got us there so fast.

Once we put our inventions safely on the ground, Aaren and I shoved the platform and managed to get it stuck in the bushes. It wouldn't be the first time someone on a ring farther up didn't tie the platform well enough and it took an unmanned trip down the hill until it lodged itself in bushes somewhere. We grabbed our stuff, then ran the rest of the way down the tram path and through the run-off ditches just behind the shops.

Our school sat smack in the middle of town, but it wasn't just a school; it was also the community center. The gymnasium and the kitchen filled the rectangle in the middle, hallways along two sides of the rectangle led to classrooms, and as the city grew, a third side of classrooms would be added. The fourth side was city offices, with the library in one corner and Aaren's mom's medical clinic in the other corner. Not only were there potentially a lot of people at the community center, but City Circle Road surrounded the building, and everyone with a split job as a merchant had a shop on the outside of the circle. We'd have to be sneaky not to get caught. We crept between Mrs. Newberry's shoe shop and my mom's bakery. When the coast was clear, we flat-out ran toward the school.

I glanced at the clock tower that rose above the community center and groaned. We were so late! I flung open the door and we sprinted down the hall until we saw Mr. Peterson round the corner, then we walked. *Great.* I'd forgotten it was a council meeting day, which meant Mr. Peterson was here through more than just lunchtime.

Mr. Peterson's split job was to watch over the school, or to take care of "administrative issues," as the parents said. We mostly thought his job was to suck the fun out of everything. As he walked toward us, his unnaturally close eyes oozed disapproval, and his furrowed brow made his short hair stick up even more. I could tell by the look on his face that we were in trouble.

The Potato

"Sorry we're late. We—" I wanted to do a much longer apology, complete with excuses, but when his eyes flicked to my shoes, I couldn't finish.

Without looking, I knew my normally dark brown leather shoes were now tan from the thick layer of dust that surely covered them after our run. My socks were probably the exact same color. Then he looked at my bruised knees. I swear I wasn't clumsy—just active. It took a second before I realized his scrutiny wasn't focused on my knees—it was the tear in my shorts. Mr. Peterson hated when we violated dress code. I was already pushing it by wearing pants cut off at the knees, but to wear ones in such obvious need of mending was unforgivable. Then his focus went to my untucked shirt. I was sure to get detention.

His eyes shifted to the invention in my hands. I moved it a little to the center, just so he could see it better. Even though they felt the same, most people in town weren't as blatant as Mr. Peterson when they showed their disapproval of someone who, like me, didn't contribute to the town. Or their delight in someone who, like Aaren, contributed tons. I always tried to do what everyone expected—it just hadn't worked out as well for me as it had for everyone else. Mr. Peterson scowled at my invention, probably thinking of all my past failures. I waited for his scowl to change when he saw that this invention was a good one, but it didn't.

When he looked at my face, I wore my sweetest smile, but he didn't even notice. I held my breath and waited for him to say something. Maybe he stayed quiet to worry us more.

Mr. Peterson's gaze turned from me to Aaren, and in that split second the disappointment and annoyance left his face.

Aaren's appearance hadn't held up any better than mine. He looked like I'd expect him to look after careening down a hill—his hair stuck out in all directions, tangled, his dark blue shirt was only half tucked in, and his shoes and the bottom of his pants looked dusty, too. But he stood straight, shoulders back, and wore his serious face, the one that only disappeared when we weren't around adults. I knew adults liked his attitude, but I also knew that wasn't the main reason he got more pleased looks from Mr. Peterson. It was because of what he held under his arm.

Aaren cleared his throat. "Good morning, Mr. Peterson. My invention gave me troubles." He held it up, as if it had caused the whole problem. "Sorry it made us late."

I exhaled more than I meant to. The whole time, I'd been trying to keep Aaren and Brenna out of trouble, but Aaren was going to get us all out of trouble in three seconds flat. As grateful as I was, it still stung that he could get away with so much more than I could.

Mr. Peterson narrowed his eyes at me, as if Aaren had said, *It was all Hope's fault we were late. She's the one to blame.* Okay, maybe it *was* all my fault. But Mr. Peterson didn't know that. He was just being judgmental.

Eventually Mr. Peterson turned his back to me and crouched down to Brenna's height. "Good morning, Brenna. How are you?"

"Very well, thank you," Brenna said. "Good morning, Mr. Peterson!"

The part of her sandy hair that wasn't windblown and frizzy fell in ringlets down to her shoulders. She was small for a five-year-old, so the blue cotton shirt tucked into her

21

pants was just as small as the four-year-olds' in her class. Her blue eyes beamed up at Mr. Peterson. It was impossible not to love Brenna. Especially since, like her entire family, she showed inventing promise.

Mr. Peterson stood back up. "You better get your sister to class."

"I'll take her right now," Aaren said. Even though Aaren was a perfectionist, he knew he wasn't perfect. I knew he wasn't perfect. But at this time of year, the rest of the town thought he was. I couldn't get out the apology or the excuse. Aaren gave both, *and* somehow got Mr. Peterson to not give us detention. It was amazing what a reputation for inventing could do for you and your best friend.

Mr. Peterson gave a nod. "Get there quickly."

Aaren took a couple of steps toward Brenna's classroom, and I'd just taken my first step when Mr. Peterson said, "Not yet, Miss Toriella."

I froze, and Aaren stopped in his tracks. Mr. Peterson tapped his foot. "Aaren had a problem with his invention?"

I nodded, not knowing what to say.

"So," Mr. Peterson said, "why, then, are *you* late?"

"Um . . . I was helping?"

Mr. Peterson glanced at my invention, then looked back at my face. "We come to class on time and without violating dress code *yet again*, Miss Toriella, or we get detention.

For the next two weeks, you better wake up extra early to get your morning chores done, because you'll be on the eight a.m. train here to clean bathrooms."

I had barely opened my mouth to protest when he cut me off. "Get to class now," he said as his eyes flicked down to my invention, "before I decide that your detention will start during inventions class today."

Mr. Peterson didn't hang around to see my reaction—he just strolled away. I kicked at the floor. It was so unfair! He just assumed my invention was bad again—without even noticing how hard I'd worked on it. And to give me bathroom detention was *extra* mean! For everyone else, detention meant cleaning chalkboards or sweeping classrooms. He gave me the only job that rivaled cleaning chicken coops.

Aaren took the couple of steps back in my direction and looked down the hall at Mr. Peterson, then at me. "I'm sorry."

"It's fine. I don't mind cleaning bathrooms," I lied. "Thanks for trying to get me out of trouble."

"He shouldn't have given you detention," Brenna huffed. "It wasn't your fault!"

"I *was* late and I *did* violate dress code."

"Yeah, but he . . ." Aaren trailed off.

I finished his sentence for him. "Really gave me detention because I stink at inventing?"

"But you don't," Aaren said. "Your invention is great."

A calmness poured over me. He was right—my invention was pretty great. I looked down at the wood base on my invention that I had spent hours and hours sanding. Even the corners felt smooth in my hands. And after learning by trial and error so many ways not to tie cords, the lashing on the upper parts turned out perfectly. Once my invention was shown at the Harvest Festival Inventions Contest and everyone saw how great it was, Mr. Peterson and everyone else would treat me differently.

I pulled my schoolbag around to my stomach, but when I put my hand on the front of the bag, I didn't feel the lump I expected and my calm turned to panic. "My potato!" I gently set my invention on the ground, then dumped my bag upside down, spilling everything on the floor of the hall. I rummaged through the contents, hoping the potato somehow hid with my small chalkboard, half a dozen pieces of chalk, and the book I had wrapped up in a protective cloth.

It wasn't there.

It felt like butterflies made of fire flapped around my insides. I ran to the door and looked outside. My breath came in shallow gasps as my eyes searched frantically along the direction we came, hoping to see the lump that could be my potato.

Nothing.

It probably fell out when I got off the tram. I almost took off running to get it, but Mr. Peterson's warning echoed in my head. *Get to class now, before I decide that your detention will start during inventions class today.* If I left, I wouldn't get to show my invention at all.

Aaren grabbed my arm. "It's okay, Hope. We'll go see Mrs. Davies in the lunchroom. She'll give us one."

Of course that solution made sense to Aaren. If he'd made my invention, a different potato would have worked fine. I shook my head. "I had to search through hundreds of potatoes to find one that'd work."

"We'll find one," he said in a voice convincing enough to give me a shred of hope.

As Aaren walked Brenna to class, I raced into the kitchen and barely skidded to a stop before I knocked into the back of Mrs. Davies. She was well into her seventies, yet still spent hours each day at school, because every kid needs "a hug and a lunch come midday." She was one of the original citizens of the town—the ones who were alive when the green bombs hit—and was the oldest person in White Rock. She turned and smiled at me, her wrinkles crinkling all the way up to her eyes. Then she noticed my frantic state.

"What can I help you with, sweetie?"

"I need a potato," I managed to squeak out with the small amount of breath my lungs held.

Her wrinkles sagged. "Oh, honey, I don't have many. I peeled them for lunch today, and the only ones left are ones I didn't think these hands could manage." She held up her bent hands apologetically. "I think there's only three left."

Wednesday meant fried potatoes for lunch. Most Wednesdays I did my farm chores as quickly as possible so I could take the eight a.m. train to school to help Mrs. Davies peel them. Today, though, I chose to jump into the Bomb's Breath. The sight of her hands made me wish I'd come to the lunchroom instead.

"I'm sorry I didn't help," I said, the guilt growing in my chest.

Mrs. Davies wiped her hands on a towel. "Don't you worry. I missed your company, but I know you got other things you gotta do. Now, let's see about getting you a potato."

I set my invention on the counter and opened the bin, which held three of the saddest potatoes I'd ever seen. They must have grown in a bed of rocks where they didn't have space to grow normally, because they looked like they had tried to sprout potato fingers. I had to have something, so I picked the one closest to the size I needed and turned around just as Aaren came through the door.

He looked at my face, then at the potato in my hand, and forced a smile. "Come on. It'll be okay."

I gave Mrs. Davies one last apology, swore I'd show up next Wednesday if I could finish cleaning the bathrooms in time, then cradled my invention in one hand and the potato in the other as we headed to class. Aaren was right. It would all be okay. After working so hard for so long to prove myself, it couldn't all go wrong because of one measly potato.

Relics
4

When I walked into my history class, I could barely take my eyes off the front of the room long enough to put my invention on the back counter with the projects from the rest of the class members. I didn't know what made me happier—seeing Mr. Allen seated up front, or the table full of relics next to him.

Mr. Allen was everyone's favorite teacher, so when we found out he had Shadel's Sickness just before Harvest Break four and a half weeks ago, almost the entire class had cried. Mr. Allen had spent the whole month of Harvest Break in bed, recovering. Wherever his skin wasn't red and blotchy, it was pale, and he looked weak.

But he was alive.

Aaren and I slid into our seats. It was obvious that everyone's enthusiasm about inventions had made class start late, because Mr. Allen was just leading the class in our motto, which usually happened right at the beginning.

"Class, why do we need to learn about history?"

Everyone answered in unison, "So we don't repeat the same mistakes."

Mr. Allen had asked the same question every day since we began this class in January, and we answered the same. I know he meant to stress the importance of history, but it always sounded to me like a challenge. And I liked a challenge.

We finished Tens & Elevens learning about World War II, but Mrs. Kearney hated questions, so I had lots left from last year when we got into Mr. Allen's class. That first day, I asked Mr. Allen the question that had bothered me the most—why they would build a bomb so much more powerful than the bombs of World War II, when they'd already seen the destruction the older bombs caused. It was like they hadn't learned anything.

Mr. Allen said they did learn things—they just anticipated wrong on some things, and hoped for the best on others.

"For example," he said, "they learned not to build a bomb that would damage the environment, like the atomic bombs did. They went to great lengths to make the green bomb 'green.' We have those scientists to thank for this incredibly fertile valley we live in."

It was true. My grandpa said the only people who survived the bombs were underground and far away from where any bomb hit. My grandparents and twenty-four others found one another and searched for a place to start over, gathering every stray animal they came across along the way. They were so happy when they discovered White Rock's crater, the tunnel leading inside that the White Rock River flowed through, and everything green growing around and inside the crater. They knew they'd found home, even before Mr. Hudson, our town's super-inventor, did tests to make sure the land and vegetation were safe.

It felt weird to thank the scientists for making our farming life easier, though, when they helped cause the deaths of nearly everyone in the world. I was about to bring up that point when Mr. Allen said, "You have to understand the situation they were in. General Shadel had risen in power and convinced his government that they had a legitimate claim to rule neighboring countries. His leaders gave him authority to invade. He and his army overtook the first country quickly, and he overthrew his own government even more quickly.

"General Shadel was both feared and respected as he set his sights on other countries he felt he had a claim to.

Nations began to pick sides—either to join him or to try to stop his invasions. With his charisma, General Shadel gained many allies by making promises of a better world for all who supported him, even though that *better world* meant being ruled by a tyrant. Battle lines spanned three continents. Casualties numbered in the millions, with a threat of world domination from General Shadel on the horizon." Mr. Allen shrugged. "Our side had to do something. Since the Worldwide Nuclear Disarmament Act eighteen years earlier, we didn't have a weapon that could force General Shadel to back down. It sounds ironic now, but we developed the green bomb in order for the people of the world to survive. We thought that with the green bomb, we could win."

Like Mr. Allen said, we anticipated wrong.

I stared at the two maps hanging on the wall behind Mr. Allen. The detailed one from before the bombs with all the cities and states and countries clearly marked, and the one from now, where cities had been drawn in by hand in a few places but most of the map was blank.

The second day of class, I raised my hand again. "Mrs. Kearney said that after we got nuclear bombs, lots of other countries did, too. Why'd the scientists think they could build an even better bomb and no other countries would copy them?"

Mr. Allen nodded. "They knew it was a possibility—

they just didn't expect it to happen so fast. In 2069, we moved our scientists to a secluded city they hoped was isolated enough. Anyone know where that city was?" He blinked a few times, like he couldn't believe we hadn't been taught that yet. "It was here, in Cook, Nebraska. Apparently it wasn't isolated enough. Somehow plans were leaked to General Shadel's scientists, and by the time we had a prototype, so did they. At that point, it became a race to see who could arm themselves with green bombs the fastest. We had hoped for the best and got the worst."

We knew the rest of the story. Our side led General Shadel to believe that we were further behind in making the bombs than we actually were. Everyone assumed there would be negotiations, and that the general would demand we surrender. He didn't negotiate. Instead, he fired the green bombs on us and our allies. Nine of them destroyed the entire United States.

He fired his other eighteen green bombs on our allies.

During the few minutes after General Shadel fired the bombs but before they hit us, all the news stations told everyone to get to a bomb shelter if they had one, while we fired our thirteen bombs on him and his allies. We made sure the first one hit right where we knew the general was stationed.

I looked at the circles on the map that were our history teachers' best guesses of where each bomb hit. A circle represented the two-hundred-mile radius around each bomb where everything was decimated—people, animals, technology, buildings—and a much larger circle represented the area where everyone on the surface was killed but a few ruins of cities remained. There was no place where the bigger circles didn't overlap.

But today Mr. Allen wasn't talking about World War III, the bombs, or General Shadel. He was talking about the inventions that existed before all that. "Before the bombs," he said, "there were a million inventions people used every day that we no longer have."

Mr. Allen motioned to the table next to him. There were a few things I had seen before in the library or in other classes, but some of them I had no idea about.

I loved seeing relics. But just like we gathered into groups and formed towns, bandits gathered into groups and stole from towns. It was dangerous to search for relics left over from before the bombs, and to transport them all the way back to White Rock, so we didn't have many.

"Since everyone seems to be in the mood for inventions today, we're going to be talking about the technology revolution of the twenty-first century."

He reached out and grabbed something silver and shiny about three inches by two inches, and about a half inch thick. There was a strange circle thing on the front of it, and the back was mostly black, and buttons and knobs were all over it but they were almost flat against the metal. "Anyone know what this is?"

Along with the rest of the class, I shook my head. Everything on it was so small. Even the words printed on it or carved into it were minuscule.

Nate Vanlue raised his hand. "A cell phone?"

A cell phone! I'd heard of those. They let people talk over long distances. Aaren's brother Travin said they didn't just carry voices, though. He said they contained images and books and music and moving pictures and games and news, but I didn't believe him. I heard they were teeny.

"Nope. Any other guesses?" When no one raised a hand, he told us. "It's a camera." I had heard of a camera before, too, but I'd never seen one. Mr. Allen picked up a book from the table and thumbed through it. "A camera could be used to take a picture of anything. Like this." He held open a page that showed hundreds and hundreds of people sprawled out in a field, listening to people play musical instruments.

Mr. Allen showed us a cylinder called a flashlight. Then he passed around a flat object about a foot square that had individual twists of something that looked like short pieces of thick string sticking up, but it was so much softer than any string I'd ever felt. He said it was called carpet, and that it used to cover the floors in people's homes. When it was my turn, I just laid my cheek on the soft fibers and imagined an entire room of it. Then he showed us a picture of my favorite thing—a machine that actually washed your dishes for you!

And the best thing about the inventions before the bombs was that there were enough people—thousands and thousands in every city—so not everyone had to invent. Only the people who were really good at it invented, and only because they wanted to. It was strange to think that if World War III hadn't happened, I'd be living with the kinds of technology he showed us.

It was even stranger that people I knew had used that stuff—all the twenty-six original members of White Rock. Since Mr. Allen was the first person born in White Rock, he was also the oldest person here who hadn't used any of those inventions. The more Mr. Allen told us about the things that once existed, the more I understood why everyone placed such importance on inventing. They wanted that technology back.

But it wasn't going to happen.

When the green bombs hit, they left behind side effects. Besides new plants, metals having different properties, weather patterns changing, and the existence of the Bomb's Breath, the green bombs destroyed any ability to create a stable magnet. No magnets meant no electric motors. And no electric motors meant no to a lot of the inventions they had back then. The people in White Rock have invented some pretty great things, but no matter what we did, we'd never get back to the technology level that existed before the bombs. It meant inventing was more difficult now than it used to be.

But just because it was difficult didn't mean I was willing to give up.

Inventions Day

As soon as history was over and I walked into the inventions classroom, excitement buzzed through my veins. There were 917 people living in White Rock, and everyone four and older made an invention for the Harvest Festival competition. That was a *ton* of inventions. I hoped mine wouldn't get lost in the masses. I wanted everyone to see it.

The clock read 11:05, with Helen Johnson's name displayed on the plaque below it. I imagined a plaque somewhere with my name on it. Maybe my potato-peeler invention would be installed in the school kitchen, and Mrs. Davies would use it all the time. Maybe people would even use it in their homes. Maybe we would use it in *my* home.

I grabbed hold of my necklace. The pendant was from my birth mom, but the chain was from my parents. It was silver and woven so intricately, it reminded me of the woven pastry my mom baked only once a year on my birthday. The chain was made long before the green bombs and was the most beautiful thing I'd seen in my whole life. I ran my finger down its smooth surface and thought of my parents. I was going to make them proud!

My inventions teacher, Mrs. Romanek, stood at the front of the classroom with an anxious face. Mr. Hudson, our town's super-inventor, sat on a tall wooden stool next to her, his foot resting on the bottom rung, which was still charred from my first and last attempt at doing a chemical experiment two years ago. The black case he always carried lay on a table behind him. Mr. Hudson came to every grade each year on Inventions Day to see all the Harvest Festival projects. He was so good at inventing and figuring things out, he was the only person in all of White Rock who didn't have a main job of farming and a split job of teaching, running a shop, mining, being a doctor, or something like that. His main job *and* his split job were inventing and teaching. Mr. Hudson had a kind smile, and eyes that always sparkled like something thrilling was happening in his head. Today he wore a dark blue suit, probably for the council meeting this afternoon.

Mr. Hudson looked amused as he watched my noisy class, but Mrs. Romanek wasn't happy at all. She held her grade book in one hand and rubbed her forehead with her thumb and two fingers as we all crowded into the room.

"Quiet!" she called over the clamor, and narrowed her don't-test-me eyes at each of us. "Class, this is a busy week. I know you're excited about showing your inventions today, the field trip tomorrow, and then the Harvest Festival. We're wasting time, though! It'll take most of class—before and after lunch—to get through everyone's inventions, so put yours on your desk and find a spot against the walls to watch."

This classroom was almost twice as big as our history classroom, and the half that wasn't filled with desks was filled with equipment for working with chemicals, machinery for shaping wood and metal and even glass, and several bookcases of old reference books. Aaren sat his invention on the desk in front of me, and my cousin and second best friend, Carina, sat hers on the desk to my right.

Carina and I were cousins, but since I was adopted, we didn't share any genes. And it was obvious. My dark hair hung stick-straight and thick, while her blond hair fell in soft waves down to her shoulders. My eyes were brown; hers were blue. My skin looked like I spent all day in the sun, while hers was pale. I liked to do daring things; she liked to talk. Carina wore pants, and mine were cut into shorts, but otherwise we dressed almost identically. She looked much more girlish than I did.

We still had fun together, though. I wished I could tell her about my morning, but she didn't know we ever jumped through the Bomb's Breath. Like everyone else, merely mentioning it made her twitchy.

As I carried my invention, I almost dropped it when someone knocked into me. I knew before I even turned to see him place his invention on the desk in front of Carina that it was Brock. He might keep to himself, but he always let me know when he was nearby—usually with a shove, a punch in the arm, or a stomp on my foot.

Aaren, Carina, and I walked to a wall together and sat down. Aaren and I were starting to be friends with Brock, but it was still hard to figure out if Brock wanted to join us or not. He pushed his way past some people and sat beside Carina. I guess today he did want to. With such strong, squarish shoulders, Brock seemed confident, but half the time his shoulders drooped, like worries weighed them down. And then there was the way his almost-black hair fell to his green eyes that made him look shy. I could never figure out which he really was—shy or worried or confident. He pushed the hair off his forehead and leaned against the wall. *Confident.* Smug, even.

It made me want to gloat about the jump I made. As soon as I opened my mouth to speak, though, Mrs. Romanek said, "Sam Beckinwood. Please come show us your invention."

I stared at Brock until he looked at me. I kept my eyes on his as I dramatically pulled out the band that held my hair, then grabbed my ponytail with one hand and swept the fallen hair back into it with the other hand. I did it as slowly and meaningfully as possible, but it still took him a moment to catch on to why my hair had been such a mess.

I could tell the second he figured out that I'd completed the double front flip, because he sat straight up and looked away from me. Not before I saw frustration on his face, though.

It felt like victory all over again. *Brock Sances,* I thought as I leaned back and smiled, *who's wearing the smug look now?*

My smile didn't fade as I tuned in to Sam explaining his invention. He said it was his farm's turn to grow peas this year, and he hated to shell them. He placed five peapods, unopened, each into a separate shaft of the invention he held. With his other hand, he pushed a lever and all five pods opened and the peas fell into a bowl. He said he'd made a bigger one at home, one that would do twenty pods at once. Mrs. Romanek and Mr. Hudson asked a few questions, gave a suggestion, and told him he did a great job.

Everyone in class cheered for him, especially me. It had been our turn for peas two years ago, and since then I'd always felt bad for anyone who was assigned peas.

Mrs. Romanek and Mr. Hudson walked to the second desk and called Ellie Davies. Ellie picked up the metal case on her desk, then opened it to reveal a bunch of cylinders. She explained how the metal case clamped on to the pipes that came from the water tanks behind our fireplaces, and as the warm water passed through the pipes, it heated the cylinders. She said she then wrapped the cylinders in her hair until they cooled, and it made her hair curly.

"I used to have to put curlers in my hair when it was wet," Ellie said, "and then wear them to bed. It's so hard to sleep in curlers! With my invention, you can put them in dry hair, and it only takes a few minutes to curl. As you can see"—Ellie bobbed her head to make her curls bounce—"they work perfectly!"

Mrs. Romanek smiled, complimented Ellie, suggested a way she could alter the clamp to make it sturdier, then moved on.

That was pretty much how it went at every desk. Each student was called over, showed his or her invention, got praise and suggestions, then everyone clapped. As they worked closer to my desk, I got more and more excited. We saw Paige Davies's machine for separating the grain

from the chaff using beaters and a bellows, Holden Newberry's model of an adjustable boat propeller that made
steering into the pier on the river easier, and Nate Vanlue's loud bell attached to a clock that rang when class
was over.

With as much training as we'd had, everyone in my
class was good at inventing, and some of them excelled at
it. This was the first year I hadn't been dying to ask one of
them for help. Every project we'd done since January had
been in teams, but we were on our own for our Harvest
Festival inventions. *No one* could get help, not even kids in
Fours & Fives. The Harvest Festival was a celebration of
how much a single person could contribute, and everyone
in town respected the rules. No one even asked their parents for help, because they knew they wouldn't get it.

Twenty minutes remained before lunch when Aaren
was called over to explain his invention. He showed an
ancient-looking book from the town library about combin-
ing chemicals. "This has great recipes for medicines, but
they all have to be cooked to an exact temperature. So I
made a thermometer. I got some metal from the smith and
coiled it at the bottom. When I put the thermometer in the
liquid, it heats the coil, which turns the shaft hooked to the
pointer. It took trial and error to get it calibrated, but now
I can measure the temperature when I cook." He gave his

I'm-talking-about-science-and-people-are-listening grin. It was such a happy grin, it made me feel bad that I didn't listen to him talk about science more often.

"I made these yesterday when I used my thermometer while heating two chemicals." Aaren grabbed a handful of some crystals from a bowl and held them out for us to see. Then he dropped them back into the bowl, ground them with a pestle, and showed us the powder. "When I mix this powder with a liquid to make a gel, it becomes a medicine that will keep infection away from cuts better than any herbs we use now."

Mrs. Romanek looked as proud as if she'd come up with the invention herself.

Mr. Hudson gave a nod of approval, and said, "Aaren, you did a great job of . . . what, class?"

We all yelled in unison, just like we did when he was our inventions teacher in Tens & Elevens, "Working with your strengths!" And then we all cheered.

"Hope Toriella," Mrs. Romanek called out. "Come show us yours."

This was the beginning of inventions going well for me. Everyone quieted and sat at attention because they were excited to see my new invention, not like in years past where they watched to see how I'd fail. I walked over to my desk and picked up my knotted potato and cleared my throat. "My mom cooks potatoes almost every night, and it's my job to peel them. I hate it, so I made an invention to do it for me."

My hands trembled as I picked up my potato with one hand and a stick with the other. I had sharpened one end of the stick and attached a handle to the opposite end. After a slow, calming breath, I steadied my hand and pushed the stick all the way through the potato until the sharp part poked out the other end. I carefully laid the potato between two forked pieces of wood I had nailed to either end of the flat base, both ends of the stick lying cradled on the forked parts. The potato came remarkably close to resting against the knife I'd lashed to a stick on the side, and I smiled. My theory was, as I turned the handle of the sharp stick, it would turn the potato, and as it rubbed against the knife, the knife would cut the potato skin off.

The thing about theories, though, is that real life doesn't always follow them. Sometimes you lose your perfect potato on the way to school.

I'd spent two weeks trying to make the knife move so it would work with different-sized potatoes, but I wasn't good at making things with my hands. If I'd used all the fancy machinery our inventions teachers had taught us to use over the years, my project wouldn't look any better—I would probably just have fewer than ten fingers now.

t'll still work. I took a deep breath and turned the ndle as I pushed the potato forward. One twist of my wrist, and the potato didn't touch the knife at all. The second twist of my wrist actually worked well. I relaxed my shoulders and smiled.

I pushed the potato in a bit farther and gave the handle another twist. One of the knobby parts of the potato that rivaled my dad's thumbs for size and sturdiness twisted from underneath and knocked the knife upward. I didn't even have time to react, so I was still pushing when the knob cleared the knife. With the force of my push, the potato part went forward too far, the forked sticks splintered, and the handle flew out of my hand. It, along with the potato, skidded across the cement floor and came to rest right in front of Ellie.

I couldn't move—I could only stare at the potato, and then down at where a sharp splinter of wood had lodged itself in my palm. My vision blurred as I stared at the bead of blood that slowly oozed out of my wound.

Silence crowded the room. Awkward silence. Unnerving silence. Eventually I pulled my eyes to what was even more painful than my hand—my broken potato peeler.

Mrs. Romanek looked from my invention to me, then glanced at Mr. Hudson like she was embarrassed he was in the room to witness such a spectacular failure of one of her students.

"Sometimes inventions don't work out like you planned." Mr. Hudson smiled his kind smile, like he understood I'd tried my best. I blinked back tears and tried to swallow the emotion pushing its way up. Not only had Mr. Hudson been my inventions teacher for two years, but he'd come to every Inventions Day since I was four. He knew my history with inventing. And at that moment, it felt like a history that was impossible to change.

"Hope," Mrs. Romanek said.

I looked away from Mr. Hudson and tried to focus on my teacher. "Yes?"

"We've talked about Harvest Festival projects for months! The concept drawings I approved were better than this. And you had four weeks to work on it during Harvest Break! Did you just blow it off and throw something together at the last minute?"

Actually, it had been longer than the two months we'd worked on the project in class. I'd been planning my invention triumph since last year, when my weed-pulling invention turned disastrous. Every pair of eyes in the room focused on me, and my face burned. Was it worse to tell her I'd worked on it for so long, or would I look less stupid if I said I did it last night? In the end, honesty won out and I blurted, "I tried really hard!"

Mrs. Romanek shook her head and looked down. I couldn't tell if she was more disappointed in me or in herself for not producing better results from a student. After what seemed like an eternity, she looked up and met my eyes. "I'm sorry, Hope, but I can't allow this"—she gestured toward my pile of sticks—"at the inventions show. You won't be able to enter an invention this year."

It felt like the ceiling collapsed on me, and all I could hear was the shocked gasps from my classmates. I stumbled toward the others, dropped to the floor, and told myself it didn't matter. But I didn't believe myself. Of course it mattered! And not just to Mrs. Romanek and Mr. Hudson, or to my dad, or for my grade—it mattered more than anything else to *everyone*. And I couldn't do it.

"Carina Toriella," Mrs. Romanek called out, her voice sounding a world away.

The pulsing of the blood in my brain was so strong and my insides were so hot, I couldn't hear anything going on around me. I stared out the high window at the Shovel—a rock formation at the very top of the mountain that looked like a shovel without its handle—which marked the direction we went to sky jump. I wanted to go there, above the Bomb's Breath, where I could escape everything. Where goals I spent months working on didn't fall apart with one wrong twist of my wrist.

When Carina finished showing her invention, she sat next to me and put her hand on my knee. "It's okay, Hope. I'm sure you're not the only one bad at inventing."

Maybe I wasn't. But it definitely felt like I was the worst. Like everyone else was at least good enough.

For the rest of the day, even when I pretended the crushing weight wasn't there, it was. Dragging me down. Keeping me from eating lunch and from seeing the other half of the class's inventions after lunch. For probably the first time ever, I wished my last class—math and English—wouldn't end. I wished Mrs. Vanlue would talk for hours.

Because then I wouldn't have to go to the council meeting and see my dad, and tell him that I failed.

Again.

My Dad

The crowds of people at the council meeting distracted me from my gigantic case of *poor me*. Council meetings started as soon as school let out, and tons of people came—usually several hundred packed themselves into the school's gym. But today even more people than usual were in attendance. Mr. Hudson planned to present an invention idea to the council, and he only did that when an invention was life-changing. Rumors had spread all week about what it might be.

Aaren and I didn't sit with most of the kids on the floor at the front—we stood halfway back and leaned against the wall on the right side of the gym, with Brenna on Aaren's shoulders. It was easier to watch everyone's reactions and still see my dad, who was sitting on the raised platform.

Mr. Hudson stood up to address the council, opened his black case on the council table, and took out a pointer. I wasn't the only one who looked up to him. In a city like ours, Mr. Hudson was royalty. Because of him, we had a steam plow, ammonia refrigeration systems at the livestock farms, a telegraph system powered by electrolyte batteries, and a lot of things people used every day.

He'd been only twelve years old when the bombs hit. Even at that age—*my* age—he loved science. Before the bombs, his parents built a bunker that happened to be deep enough and far enough from a bomb to protect them, and he'd filled it with every science and math book he could get his hands on. A lot of the books in the town library and all the ones our inventions teachers used came from Mr. Hudson's stash.

Through the crowd I saw my mom sitting next to Aaren's mom on the front row of benches. A couple dozen aunts, uncles, and cousins sat scattered throughout the hundreds of people who filled the gym. And one dog. Sandy sat next to Mr. Williams on a bench, like she was a person.

I scanned the crowd, watching body language and facial expressions. Sometimes when the council talked about a change, everyone reacted the same. Other times it was half and half. Today was a great day to watch—crowd reactions were exactly in unison. Mr. Hudson announced he had found a way for every home to have refrigeration. Since refrigerators were pretty much at the top of everyone's wish list, his announcement caused a wave of excited whispers through the crowd.

He pointed at a complicated drawing on an easel, cleared his throat, then said, "The air in the Bomb's Breath is a resource, and it can be tapped for our advantage. The cross-linking of its molecules creates pressure. When we bring air down from the Bomb's Breath through pipes, the pressure of it going through a small orifice and then expanding again will power the refrigeration. Pipes at the other end of the unit right here will then vent the air back into the Bomb's Breath."

The second he mentioned the Bomb's Breath, the crowd fell silent. A moment later, they started whispering again. The volume in the room grew louder and louder as Mr. Hudson spoke. Council member Mr. Newberry's face actually got redder than his hair, and he squeezed his pencil like he was trying to choke it. To his credit, he did wait until Mr. Hudson finished before he exploded.

"I can*not* believe you are proposing we bring air from the Bomb's Breath down here," Mr. Newberry yelled. "And into our homes! Do you want us all to die? Do you want your kids to die? Your wife? How about your *dad*?"

That last one gave me chills. Mr. Newberry's dad was the person who found out the Bomb's Breath was deadly almost forty years ago. The hard way. While cataloging plants that grew in the mountains, he walked right into the Bomb's Breath, not knowing it even existed, and it killed him. It happened only a couple of months before Mr. Newberry was born. I understood why he was mad, but we all knew Mr. Hudson would never suggest something unsafe.

"No one will die." Mr. Hudson pointed to his chart. "See? The air will stay contained."

Mr. Newberry shook his head. "And if it doesn't?" He looked to the other members of the council. "It's too risky! Especially when we already have refrigeration."

The noise level in the gym rose even higher, but Mr. Hudson kept his voice impressively calm. "The refrigeration we have isn't adequate. We have enough for the livestock farms, true, but we've already decided it requires too much fuel to put one in every home." He pointed to his chart. "This invention runs itself, and it taps into a self-renewing resource. The Bomb's Breath."

Mrs. Beckinwood, the council head and one of the oldest original citizens of White Rock, pursed her lips, wrote something on a piece of paper, then passed it down the table to my dad.

Mrs. Williams, who always wore her hair in a bun on council days, cleared her throat. "There's another problem. The Bomb's Breath is dangerous to outsiders as well as us. It's not just a curse; it's a blessing. It's one of the reasons we continue to live here. Scouts report more and more groups of bandits attacking towns. Bergen and Hayes to our south and Arris to our north have all been hit in the past month. And not just smaller towns that are less protected like Hayes and Arris, or towns farther away like Bergen. Browning has had its farms looted several times this year alone, and a large group of bandits even attacked their people last week during the harvest.

"These bandits cannot come over the mountain and attack us *because* of the Bomb's Breath. We don't want to do anything that might jeopardize that. Right now, there's only one easily guarded way in and out of our city. The Bomb's Breath is, essentially, the rest of our guard. We become vulnerable without it."

People didn't bother to whisper anymore. The fear in the room was thick, like we all breathed it in.

"Quiet down," Mrs. Beckinwood ordered. Her voice had gotten more shaky and feeble lately, so not many people heard her until she pounded her gavel on the table. She waited for the room to quiet. "David. You have something to add?"

My dad stood up, completely at ease in front of the town. Mrs. Beckinwood made a good choice in asking him to speak. I've heard that people followed my dad around, ready to do whatever he said, from the time he was in Fours & Fives. My dad's split was running the lumber mill, and he was good with his hands and liked to make inventions with wood. But most of his inventions for the Harvest Festival had to do with leading the town—like processes on how to run things more effectively.

I'd seen my dad calm an overreacting crowd before. He stood up and strode around the table to Mr. Hudson's chart. He might have been Mr. Hudson's height, but the width of his shoulders made him look intimidating. Or they would have if he didn't always wear a smile and look like he was seconds away from wrapping you in a bear hug. It could just be the way I saw him, but I think everyone noticed my dad's never-ending supply of kindness.

He laughed, a deep, throaty chuckle that caught everyone off guard. The tension in the room was cut in half as my dad's laughing filled it all the way to the corners. He clapped his hand on Mr. Hudson's shoulder twice. "Tom, you can always find a way to excite the room. And we all completely trust you and your inventions. You've not steered us wrong in forty years."

The frustration on Mr. Hudson's face eased.

My dad gestured toward the council members. "Debra and Ken brought up some valid concerns. Are there experiments you can do to make sure that both the air we breathe and the stability of the Bomb's Breath aren't compromised?"

It was a weird question for my dad to ask. My dad and I

knew Mr. Hudson would never have brought his invention to the council without doing those experiments first. Mr. Hudson turned to the council. "With the council's permission, I'll rerun the necessary tests."

I leaned against the wall and smiled. My dad had complimented Mr. Hudson so he wouldn't be defensive. He'd reminded the audience that Mr. Hudson always looked out for us. He'd made the council members feel their concerns were addressed. He'd caused a delay by requesting the tests, so people could either get used to the idea of using the Bomb's Breath as a power source or forget about it. But I knew what my dad thought of the Bomb's Breath, and I knew what everyone else thought of it. None of them would *ever* get used to the idea.

Watching my dad at work was one of the reasons I liked council meetings. Everyone always said he should run for council head, that he'd have no problem getting elected. My dad loved this town—I knew it was his dream.

But my dad wouldn't run.

I never knew why, until Amy Beckinwood from Fourteens & Fifteens cornered me in the hall a year ago on the morning of Inventions Day. She told me that she hoped my invention didn't stink as bad as every one of my past inventions did, because her grandma was old and tired and wanted to step down as council head. "She would, too," Amy had said, "but only if your dad runs for council head, because she doesn't want Mr. Newberry to win. She knows your dad wants to run, but he can't. Because of *you*."

The realization had knocked the breath out of me. She was right—how could my dad be the leader of a town that valued inventing so much, when his daughter was such an embarrassment?

The memory of last year's invention, which not only didn't work but broke the leg of the nearest desk, came back and combined with the fresh hurt of today's inventions class disaster. My nerves were raw, and suddenly I couldn't watch my dad in his element, knowing my failure not only made my dream impossible, it made *his* dream impossible.

I grabbed Aaren's arm and panted, "I have to leave."

He looked at me in alarm. "Um. Okay."

He lifted Brenna off his shoulders and put her on the floor, then glanced across the room and to the back, toward the exits. People were *everywhere*—there was no way we could get through them. Aaren nodded toward the loose paneling we'd found last year, a dozen feet behind where we stood. We weren't going to tell anyone about it, ever.

Yet here we were in a room full of people, and all I wanted to do was escape through it.

Smushed

7

Mr. Hudson sat down and Brock's grandpa, Mr. Sances, a white-haired council member with black eyebrows, stood up to introduce the next item of business. Everyone's attention turned to Harvest Festival preparations. It was possible they wouldn't even notice us moving the paneling. I nodded to Aaren.

Aaren, Brenna, and I pushed our way through the crowd and said "Excuse us" to Sam Beckinwood's dad, who was leaning against the wall. He stood up straight without taking his eyes off Mr. Sances, so we grabbed hold of the wood paneling that covered the bottom three feet of the wall and half slid, half pulled, until it opened enough for us to crawl through. We slipped into the opening with our schoolbags and shut the panel behind us.

When I took a deep breath of the dank and dusty air, I sneezed. The hole behind the paneling led into the hallway they'd built along with the gym ten years ago—the hallway would eventually lead to classrooms when the city grew enough to build them along this side, but it was completely closed off now. I was sure we were the only ones to walk down it during all that time, since the footprints in the dust were the ones we'd left during the months we'd known about it.

Aaren must have had a match in his pocket, because I heard a scrape against the cement floor, then the space filled with a dim, wavering yellow glow. At that moment, I was actually glad we didn't have lights in the ceiling like they did before the bombs, because I didn't want Aaren and Brenna to see my face any better than the match showed them.

"You okay?" Aaren whispered.

Brenna grabbed my hand with both of hers.

I nodded yes. Then no. Then yes again. "I . . ."

Aaren glanced back toward the closed paneling. "Is it your dad? Because you have to tell him about inventions class?"

I knew I couldn't talk without my voice coming out squeaky, so I nodded.

The steam whistle blew barely loud enough for us to hear through the walls, and Aaren turned his head toward the sound. "We can take the four o'clock train; then we'll have an hour before our parents expect us. Where do you want to go? We could sky jump."

I shook my head no. "I just want to go home."

My schoolbag sat in a heap at my feet. I pulled the strap over my head as I walked toward the end of the hallway, where a grate in the ceiling marked our way out. Aaren linked his hands together and I stepped on them as he boosted me to the opening. After I climbed up, I let down our rope. Aaren helped Brenna before he scaled the rope himself.

The grate led us to a three-foot-high crawl space, between the ceiling of the hall behind the gym and the roof of the building. It was small and dark, but big enough for us to crawl through. We crept along until we reached the roof's access hatch.

The roof above the classrooms and hallways was flat, but the peaked part that covered the gym hid us from the view of almost anyone who might be outside. We snuck to the corner classroom—Fours & Fives—where the clay-brick walls made it easiest to climb down. I went first; then Aaren lowered Brenna to my waiting arms. After Aaren climbed down, we had to run to make the train before the double whistle blew.

The train wasn't like trains before the bombs. The green bombs had changed the properties of steel, so now it was weak. We could make different types of metals, of course, but getting enough—even for our small steam engines that were barely big enough to hold the person manning them—was almost impossible. Besides, we didn't need big trains, just ones big enough to pull two wooden cars. Some days the cargo cars were emptied, ready to haul something to or from the upper rings, but usually benches were placed along the outsides of the flat-bottomed cars, with the two-foot-high sides holding them in place for passengers to sit.

Since the meeting was still in session, there were only four other people on the train, and two were Aaren's siblings. Aaren led us to where his older brother Travin was wrestling his three-year-old brother, Nick, onto a bench. We climbed into the same car and sat on the bench backward, our feet dangling off the sides.

"Couldn't get Nick to stay still during the meeting?" Aaren asked as the double whistle sounded.

Travin slumped his shoulders. "No. And it was a great meeting, too." He looked at Brenna, who was sitting like an angel between Aaren and me. "Why did *you* leave?"

Aaren glanced at me and shrugged. "We just didn't feel like staying."

The train jerked forward as it started to climbed up the hill. Aaren and Travin talked about Mr. Hudson's idea and the crowd's reactions. It was obvious that Travin was as afraid of the Bomb's Breath as everyone else, but he still enjoyed Mr. Hudson suggesting something that fired up the crowd so much. I ignored their chatter and stared at the passing farms, but the truth was, I could barely stay in my seat.

When the train neared our stop on the third ring, I leaned toward Aaren. "Walk home with Travin, okay?" The train had barely slowed when I leapt off and ran the rest of the way to my farm. I didn't even bother to change out of my school clothes; I just attacked my chores.

I had frustrated energy to burn, so the fact that my dad had assigned me the job of pulling out dried cornstalks actually worked well. I yanked on the stubborn stalks with all the strength I had. It was hard, but at least it wasn't like working on an invention for nothing.

I didn't stop until I knew my parents were home and dinner was ready. Exhausted in every way, I grabbed an armful of firewood and tromped into my house to the smell of the chicken stew my mom had put on to cook before the meeting.

The skirt my mom always wore to council meetings swished back and forth as she and my dad set the table. It was one of the few days of the month that I came into the house for dinner and she wasn't wearing pants and a flour-covered apron.

Unlike my dad, my mom was quiet when she was

growing up, and completely focused on baking. Everything everyone had eaten up to that point had been for survival. She changed things. She treated baking like an art form—she called it her creative outlet. Every single invention she made for the inventions show was something to help with baking—a new tool, a new method, or a new recipe.

"Hello, honey," she said as I slipped off my mud-crusted shoes. She looked me up and down, shook her head, and reached out to rub some dirt off my cheek. "You can tell you've got a whole lot of boys raising you."

My mom wasn't talking about the guard members who often helped on the farm since we had a small family. She meant my eight brothers, who died before they were even born. It comforted her to believe they hung out with me as angels and acted like real brothers would while I did my farm chores. She wasn't crazy. That was just her way of dealing with the fact that she wanted a house full of kids but only got one.

People say my mom used to be strong. She had always been thin, but each miscarriage made her a little more fragile. After the last one, where she had been far enough along we were all convinced I'd finally get a sibling, she seemed breakable. My dad wrapped his broad arms around her like a human shield and whispered something in her ear, and she laughed. I knew he'd protect her from anything. My dad told me once that he'd been in love with my mom since they were five. For twelve years she didn't have a clue.

We sat down to eat, and my parents talked of nothing but the meeting. The meeting and the dangers of the Bomb's Breath.

"Are you going to eat that stew," my dad asked, "or just swirl your spoon through it all evening?"

I forced a smile.

"Feeling guilty about being late for school this morning?" My dad's eyebrows were raised, and he had that *You didn't think I knew, did you?* look on his face.

Oh, that. I had forgotten about being late. "Sorry. We went for a walk this morning and lost track of time."

"Hope." My dad put down his spoon. "You're a leader. People follow you. That means the decisions you make affect more than just you. You need to have the good of others in mind, too."

I scoffed. "Dad, I'm *not* a leader."

My dad just looked at me for a moment. "You're more of a leader than you realize."

"He's right," my mom said. "You find yourself in any situation and instantly know what to do."

I shook my bowed head. Leaders could set goals, then work hard and actually reach them. Like my dad did. I looked up at my parents. "My invention—" My voice caught in my throat. "It was every bit as bad as last year. No, worse. This year I can't even be in the inventions show. I'm sorry."

My mom reached out and gave my hand a squeeze. I dropped my head and watched a tear fall onto my shorts.

The silence lasted a few moments longer than I could stand. Then my dad's chair legs scraped across the floor. He walked to me and lifted my chin with two of his stocky fingers.

"Hope. There's a lot more that I love about you than your inventing skills."

A laugh mixed with a sob hiccuped in my chest. I was pretty sure my dad would love me even if I had a second nose growing out of my forehead. That was just the way he was. But sometimes it was really tough being an only child. Just like my name said, all my parents' hopes were smushed into one person. Me.

I grabbed my necklace and ran my thumb down the chain. The smooth chain that didn't go with the rough stone pendant it held. I couldn't help wondering how many times my parents had wished they had a kid with their own genes, someone they could have passed on their talents to. Someone who didn't keep messing things up.

Someone who wouldn't keep my dad from running for council head.

Field Trip

My class and I followed Mr. Allen as he rode my favorite of the town's horses, Arabelle, in a slow walk to the edge of the woods, then waited for us to stop talking. We couldn't help being excited—field trips to places where we might someday work as splits were one of the best things about Twelves & Thirteens. And knowing how sick Mr. Allen was, we hadn't been sure he'd be strong enough to join us, horseback or not.

We had taken the train to the end of the third ring, and the breeze helped whip away the crawlies I felt after cleaning the bathrooms. The community center had two toilets someone had scavenged from before the bombs, but the rest were cement with polished wood seats and were much worse to clean. I shuddered just thinking about it. Stupid detention.

We stood on the mostly uninhabited side of White Rock, directly across the valley from my house. To reach the mines where the river exited the valley, we first had to travel through the woods. As everyone gathered around Mr. Allen, I patted Arabelle's neck and ran my hand down her jaw. She was the one I rode whenever my dad sent me to get a horse from the community stables to help haul wood planks for his split at the lumber mill.

Mr. Allen held up a hand for quiet. "You'll work in teams of three. As you search for Ameiphus, keep your teammates in sight. I don't want anyone getting lost or hurt." He held up a clump of moss. "Make sure the Ameiphus you find is the dark green kind with the little rounded leaves, and only take it if you can see mold growing on it. You all know the importance of finding as much as possible. So"—he smiled—"the team who finds the most Ameiphus gets out of a week of homework and will each get a turn to sit at my desk during class."

Everyone's eyes were as wide as mine. *No homework. Soft chair.*

Mr. Allen looked at the clipboard in his hand. "We'll form teams alphabetically."

I turned to Aaren and frowned. "I guess we aren't teammates. Have fun with Ellie and Paige."

I scanned my class for Brock and my cousin Carina before Mr. Allen said, "Brock Sances, you're with Carina Toriella and Hope Toriella." It wasn't like I couldn't think through the class list by threes.

"Everyone come grab a sack," Mr. Allen called out. "You'll have about an hour to search on your way through the woods. Listen for my whistle. When you hear it, you have ten minutes to meet me on the road at the other end of the woods."

Once Brock, Carina, and I stood together, I pointed to a path that would lead us downhill a bit and away from most of the groups of searchers. "Should we go this way?"

Brock eyed the area, like he was sizing up the competition, then nodded. We each found a flat rock we could use to dig the Ameiphus loose, then stepped over rocks and fallen trees and clumps of growing things, searching in the shade of every boulder and tree trunk.

We spotted a boulder as high as my waist—a perfect spot for Ameiphus to grow—and the three of us ran to it. Brock was the one who discovered the Ameiphus, and he bent to dig it out. I had hoped I'd be the first person to find one.

Brock pushed the Ameiphus into his sack, then moved

back several steps. He gave a loud *whoop,* took a running leap onto the boulder, then jumped up with his arms and legs out. With as much as he'd been showing off during the jump, he landed like it was nothing. Using both arms, he pointed at Carina and me and said, "I'm going to get more than you."

Competition on! We all took off running.

Ameiphus was one of the many side effects of the green bombs—it didn't exist before they hit. Of course, neither did Shadel's Sickness. At least thirty people got the sickness every year, but sometimes it was a lot more. It started with achy muscles and pale skin, and by the next day, your muscles seized to the point you could barely move, and your skin got covered with red splotches. Within a week, it moved to your organs and you died. There was an epidemic when I was four, and sixty-seven people came down with Shadel's in the same month, including my three living grandparents and Aaren's baby sister. It was a death sentence for all of them.

When Aaren's sister died, Dr. Grenwood said she wouldn't rest until she found a cure. Her theory was that if a new disease formed because of the bombs, then the cure did, too. Between her experience with medicine and Aaren's dad's expertise with plants, they eventually discovered that the mold that grew on the Ameiphus plant could be made into an antibiotic that cured not only Shadel's Sickness, but also a dozen other illnesses and infections. Now you didn't die if you got Shadel's Sickness—you were just extremely sick for six weeks.

My eyes darted from tree trunk to tree trunk and from rock to rock as we searched. Ameiphus grew in moist places with no sun. It wasn't something you could plant—you had to wait for it to grow on its own. The best time to find Ameiphus was in autumn, when we collected it for the entire year. Aaren's dad was worried that with the lack of rain we'd had, we wouldn't find enough this year.

Then something caught my eye. A clump of Ameiphus was growing in the crook of two branches in a tall pine tree, but the bottom branches were a dozen feet from the ground. I didn't know Ameiphus could grow that high.

The tree bark was rough enough to scale, so I set my sack of Ameiphus and my lunch next to the trunk, then hugged the tree with my arms and legs and scrambled up.

Once I got to the branch with the Ameiphus, I swung a leg over it and dug the Ameiphus free. That was when I noticed that Aaren's group had run into ours, and they were all watching me. Aaren shook his head and smiled like he did anytime I tried something dangerous that he totally expected me to try. Carina looked like she feared for my life. Brock had a gleam in his eye. I knew he'd be up a tree digging at an Ameiphus before I even got down from this one. But Paige Davies, the smallest girl in my class, just looked at me in awe. It made me smile. And it might have made me show off a bit as I swung from the branch back to the trunk.

I only found one more Ameiphus in a tree I had to climb. Now that the tree secret was out, everyone climbed the trees, even people like Paige. And of course Brock. He climbed more trees than anyone, even me.

While Brock was up in a tree, I knelt down to dig a piece of Ameiphus loose from between two roots. Carina crouched near me and nodded in Brock's direction. "Someone's in a good mood today."

I looked up at Brock and smiled. "Yeah." There was something about a competition that made him seem less worried.

"I think I know who his dad is."

"Really?" Since we first met Brock when he started living with his grandpa and coming to school in the spring, we'd been trying to figure out why he'd never been to school before then. Or why we hadn't seen him around town, at council meetings, or even at any of the festivals. We had no idea how he'd just appeared one day. Honestly, we weren't even sure who his parents were. The adults were no help, either. Six months ago, when Mr. Allen had said we were getting a new student, we were all in shock.

We'd never had a new student. Mr. Allen had told us not to make a big deal of it, and that the only important thing was making him feel welcome. I'd asked my dad, but he said it was Brock's story and if Brock wanted me to know, he'd tell me. But anytime we asked Brock, he'd turn away, change the subject, or tell us it wasn't our business.

Carina whispered next to my ear. "Remember the hermit who lives in the woods up near the warning fences? The one who only comes down during the Summer Festival?"

I nodded. A bandit attack or something before I was born had made him go crazy, and he didn't like being around people anymore.

"I think Brock's dad is the hermit," Carina said.

I couldn't remember if I'd ever heard the hermit's last name, but it might have been Sances.

"Maybe he had a son all along, and it's Brock. And that's why Brock doesn't like being around people sometimes— he's not used to it."

"Brock's pretty smart," I said. "Could a hermit have taught him so much?"

Carina shrugged like her explanation was the only one that made sense. "Why else wouldn't he talk about it? I think he doesn't want us to know his dad is nuts." She nodded knowingly, then walked off in search of Ameiphus.

I pushed the Ameiphus into my sack and looked up

the hill to where Brock was staring at me from his perch in the tree. He grabbed the branch and swung down, dangled his feet for a minute, then dropped to the ground.

Was that his secret? That his dad was the hermit?

At the sound of the whistle, my sack held four clumps of Ameiphus. Mr. Allen blew the whistle a second time, and Brock, Carina, and I emerged from the woods to meet the others on the path.

Brock hadn't even mentioned the fact that he didn't meet us to jump yesterday morning. I'd known everyone in my class for my entire life, so if someone didn't show up for something, I'd be able to guess why. I'd only known Brock for six months, though. With him, I had no idea. As soon as Carina was distracted, I whispered, "You didn't come jump with us yesterday morning."

He brushed his hair off his forehead, then looked at me out of the corner of his eye. "If I would've come, *I* would've been the first to land a double front flip."

I laughed and gave him a little shove.

It was months ago when Brock had seen us hiking to the cliff, snuck up behind us, and stayed hidden while we made a few jumps into the Bomb's Breath. When he stepped out into the open, I'd almost had a heart attack—I thought he'd tell on us for sure. He said he wouldn't if we let him jump. That took me by surprise even more than his sudden appearance did. I didn't think we'd find another person anywhere who would be willing to go near the Bomb's Breath, let alone jump into it. But he did, and we'd met him for jumps ever since. It was one of the few times I'd seen him happy. Like he wasn't weighed down with whatever made his shoulders slump.

He nodded toward my bag. "How many did you get?"

"Four," I said with a smile.

He took a few steps ahead of me. Right before he squeezed between two kids, he turned around. "I got five." He gave me a half-smile, then stepped into the crowd around Mr. Allen, out of my sight.

Ugh! I lost to Brock! It took away some of my excitement for being the first to land the double front flip, especially since he hadn't even been there to try to win.

As soon as we were all near Mr. Allen, Nate raised his hand before anyone else, as usual. "My team found six!"

Jella flipped her braid over her shoulder. "We found eight."

"Nice job!" Mr. Allen said. "Anyone get more than eight?"

Sam held up two sacks of Ameiphus. "We got nine!"

I mentally crossed off half the groups. Maybe mine could win!

Carina held up her two clumps of Ameiphus and yelled our team's total before Mr. Allen even called on her. "Eleven! We found eleven!"

"Us too!" Aaren said.

I grinned at Aaren. I couldn't believe our teams tied! I was trying to figure out how six people could each have a turn at Mr. Allen's desk in only five days, when I heard a commotion behind me. I turned to see Holden and his team crash through the bushes at the side of the road.

Holden took a few panting breaths before he managed to get out, "Fourteen!"

My hopes for a homework-free week fell.

"Congratulations!" Mr. Allen said. "I hope you enjoy spending the mornings of the next week taking turns on a cushioned chair, and the evenings doing something *other* than history homework. Now, remember what we talked about in class—choosing your split is a very important thing. You'll want to choose one you enjoy, and today you'll see what it's like at the mines. Let's go—Mr. Williams is going to show you something on this field trip that no other group has ever seen."

The Limestone Cave

9

After ten minutes of walking through the trees as they became more sparse, we entered a clearing, the edge of the lake in front of us, the mines at our right. Sandy, Mr. Williams's golden retriever, ran up to meet us. She wagged her tail as we all tried to pet her at the same time, then she ran back toward Mr. Williams, like she couldn't stand to be away from him for another second. We chased after her and sat down in front of Mr. Williams at the opening of the mine. Mr. Allen tied Arabelle to a post at the mine opening and sat down with us.

Mr. Williams scratched Sandy's ears, then folded his huge arms and smiled, which seemed to spread his thick mustache even wider. "Raise your hand if you like rocks.

Do you like to throw them, dig in the dirt with them, collect them?"

Most of us raised our hands.

"Then working in the mines might be the split for you." He brushed his hands together, and a fine white powder blew away in the slight breeze. "Here at the mines, we get to play with several different kinds of rocks every day."

Mr. Williams had us turn around to face the tunnel where the river flowed in from the other side of the valley—the only way into or out of White Rock. "You all know the green bomb made this crater, but the slope is steeper on this side of the valley." He gestured over the river to the south, where no homes were built. "Does anyone know why?"

It hadn't occurred to me *why* it was that way—it just was. A couple of kids raised their hands. Mr. Williams called on Sam.

"Is it because of the rock?"

"Very good. Most of our valley has a layer of dirt over it," he said as he pointed north, "but a large seam of rock passes through on this side. When the green bomb hit, it couldn't push the rock as far as it pushed the soil. Who can tell me what kind of rock gives White Rock River its name?"

The whole class raised their hands. Mr. Williams pointed to Ellie.

"Limestone."

"That's right. Limestone is important for a couple of reasons. It's the softest rock in this seam, so when the green bomb hit, it pushed the limestone farther than it pushed the harder rock surrounding it. If it weren't for the limestone, we wouldn't have the opening into this valley"—he pointed to the tunnel at the other end of the river—"and there wouldn't be a groove in the stone for the river to pass through. Instead of staying on the third ring, like it does now, the river would just come in through the opening and flow right down there to the middle of the valley, first flooding City Circle, and eventually filling the entire valley. Because of this seam, it flows into our little lake, which is actually just a place where the limestone seam widened considerably. It then flows through caves in the mountain and comes out the other side."

Mr. Williams led us into the mining cave with Sandy at his side. The opening was tall enough that one of us could stand on someone else's shoulders and still not hit our heads as we walked inside. The cave wasn't new to me—Aaren and I had explored it a few times when we came to the lake to swim, but always after the people who had mining as a split had gone home.

The first room was large enough that all eighteen members of my class, along with Mr. Williams, Sandy, and Mr. Allen, could fit without being squished. Mr. Williams told us how they dug out the limestone and hauled it to the ball mill, which was like a big spinner with hard rocks inside, and it ground the limestone into a powder so they could make it into cement.

Mr. Williams gestured to the cave. "The limestone seam goes right through the mountain. As we mined last month, we accidentally broke through to the river below because we didn't anticipate such a large air bubble above the river. Come on. I'll show you."

He grabbed a lantern and led us farther into the cave. Off the main room, a passageway with a slightly lower ceiling curved to the right. We followed the passage as it meandered deeper into the mountain, wide in some places, skinnier in others. Along the path, the walls were mostly limestone, with darker rocks showing through in places. As we rubbed against the walls in the skinnier hallways, a white powder covered our clothes. The narrowest hallway led into another cave room filled with sounds of the river.

"Okay, everyone, gather round," Mr. Williams said as he walked to a hole in the middle of the room. Sandy ran excitedly around the hole, then to the opening to hurry the rest of us along, then back to Mr. Williams's side.

The hole was bigger than I'd imagined. I thought it would be about the size of my fist, but it was probably three feet wide.

"Come on in. Don't be afraid," said Mr. Williams.

"This is the only place where the floor is thin, and we installed support beams below this whole area to make sure it wouldn't break more. It's safe to stand here."

We all formed a wide circle around the hole and leaned forward to see inside. It was completely dark until Mr. Williams tied his lantern to a rope and lowered it down the hole. The river rushed past only ten feet below the opening. There was an actual bank on one side of the river at least eight feet wide, but it narrowed both upstream and downstream to barely wider than the river itself. The ceiling got lower, too.

"Have you gone down the river?" I asked.

Mr. Williams shook his head. "When we set the support beams, we walked along the bank for a distance, but we turned back when it became too narrow and dangerous. We worried that in some places, the cave might only be as big as the river itself—no space above it, no space on the sides of it."

Everyone gasped as we collectively imagined being swept downstream underwater, unable to come up for a breath. He looked at us pointedly, to make sure we weren't going to try it ourselves sometime when he wasn't there. But really . . . even I didn't take *that* big a risk.

Harvest Festival

I wove through the crowd of people who milled around the dozens of mismatched tables we'd used for last night's Harvest Feast. The tables now sat under the shade tents, covered with all the inventions.

Even though there was a big crowd here every year for the Harvest Festival, I didn't think I'd ever get used to the sight of so many people gathered in one place. Sure, town meetings were crowded, but everyone who wasn't too sick to walk, crawl, or drag themselves came to the Harvest Festival. Plus, we'd welcomed nearly two hundred adults from Browning through the tunnel yesterday afternoon, so the group was massive.

I wished kids from Browning came, too. They used to, just like kids from here used to go to the Spring Festival every year in Browning. But when I was three, bandits attacked our caravan on the way home from the Spring Festival, and people died. Even kids. Now they never let us go.

Aaren, Brenna, and I wound through the maze of inventions until we found where Aaren's and Brenna's had been placed. When I woke up this morning and thought about how I was the only person over age four who didn't have an invention displayed, I actually considered not coming to the Harvest Festival. I was good at history—I would trade being good at history for being good at inventing. I was good at reading and math—I'd trade those. Or *any* subject, really, that people cared less about than inventing. For a minute, I thought about staying in bed.

But I couldn't. The bathrooms at the community center still had to be cleaned. Besides, I knew feeling sorry for myself wouldn't fix anything—it would only make me miss one of the best days of the year. I took a deep breath and forced a smile on my face just like I had earlier this morning. This was a party, and I intended to enjoy it.

Aaren grabbed my hand and pulled me to one of the tables that held inventions by adults. Someone had mixed two metal alloys, one that was unique to the mountains surrounding our valley. I tried to listen to him go on and on because it made him so excited, but once he started talking about the properties of the new metal, I tuned out. Finally, another invention caught his eye, and we moved on.

The smell of fresh-baked blackberry pies wafted across the invention tables, and my mouth began to water. Not only did Mrs. Davies make lunch for us at school every day, but she also, along with my mom and a dozen other people, made individual-sized pies each year and cooked them in solar ovens by the tables. Their smell alone made me wish we had the Harvest Festival every day. While Aaren explained yet another invention to me, I imagined myself holding one of the warm mini pies in my hands, biting into the flaky crust, and sinking my teeth into the sweet filling. By the time he finished talking, my stomach was growling.

Brenna tugged on Aaren's sleeve. "Those kids are taking toy boats down to the water. Can I go?"

"In a minute." Aaren leaned in closer to an invention.

She folded her arms and huffed. "No, now."

"I can't see the bank from here, Brenna, so I can't watch you. We'll play in a minute."

Brenna let out a defeated breath but didn't take her eyes off the river. I didn't blame her—looking at inventions was boring. I glanced over to where a few horses were penned by the wagons that had brought all the supplies to the festival and saw a flash of red hair. I knew it was Cass, a girl who had graduated from Sixteens & Seventeens last year.

Now her split officially was taking care of the horses, even though she'd been doing the job unofficially for as long as I could remember. Sometimes during the summer, Aaren and I would come up here and watch her trick-ride on Arabelle. Always Arabelle. Maybe that was why she was my favorite horse—because I saw how much fun Cass had riding her. I'd much rather hang out and talk to Cass about horses than look at inventions. But just like Brenna, I walked through them with Aaren anyway because the Harvest Festival was only once a year, and we both knew what it meant to Aaren.

I turned from one table and bumped into Amy Beckinwood. She took a step back and brushed her long brown hair off her shoulder.

"Hey, Hope. I feel so bad they wouldn't let you put your invention in the show."

Great. I'd had a stupid wish that somehow no one outside of my class knew. But Amy's brother Sam was in my class, and if Amy knew, everybody knew. At least she was being nice about it. Amy was nice only some of the time. "Thanks," I muttered.

"I mean, I'd feel *terrible* if year after year I was never able to do something worthwhile."

Okay, so I was wrong. She wasn't being nice about it.

"Amy," Aaren growled. He stepped in front of me, like he could protect me from her words.

"What?" she said way too innocently. "I'm just saying what everyone else is thinking. Besides, she's got to be used to it by now. You're used to it, right, Hope?"

If I were used to it, I probably wouldn't have had to convince myself to come to the festival this morning, or not to kick Amy in the shins right now. Luckily, something else grabbed Amy's attention. She pointed across the crowd. "What do you think's going on over there?"

Brock stood away from the main group of people, pleading with someone from Browning who I knew I'd seen before. We couldn't hear them over the noise, but Brock looked upset. The man put his hand on Brock's shoulder and said something. Brock dropped his head. After the man patted his shoulder, Brock trudged away.

"I have no idea," I said.

Amy spun toward her friends and gossiped about what had just happened.

Before I even had time to think about what I'd seen, Mr. Hudson's voice boomed and quieted the buzz of the crowd. "Gather around! It's time to announce the Inventions Contest winners."

We found Carina as everyone moved toward the performance platform where Mr. Hudson stood, bullhorn in hand. "There were some great inventions this year!" he said. "That means many people did what?"

Everyone called out, "Worked with their strengths!"

Mr. Hudson read the names of the winners in Fours & Fives and in Sixes & Sevens, then named the overall winner for lower grades. All three kids came to the front, beaming, to get their medals. The cheer from the crowd was deafening.

"And for Eights and Nines," Mr. Hudson said through the bullhorn, "the winner is Amanda Allen for her automatic chicken scratch spreader. For Tens and Elevens, the winner is Livi Johnson for her recipe for ink. And for Twelves and Thirteens"—I grabbed Aaren's hand and squeezed tight—"the winner is Brock Sances, for his bale grabber."

I looked to Aaren, and then to Carina. "Brock had a good invention?" I hadn't paid attention after mine failed.

Aaren nodded. "Yep. He did good." Then his focus went back to Mr. Hudson. I could tell he still hoped to be the overall winner for middle grades. He'd won it once before, so we both knew it was possible. I crossed my fingers for him.

"And the overall winner for middle grades is Charles Beckinwood, for his wheeled seed-planting invention."

Aaren's shoulders fell. I didn't know anyone who was more of a perfectionist than Aaren. He didn't care if something took all his free time, as long as it turned out well. Especially if it was anything science-related. I knew he felt terrible, and that made me feel terrible.

"I'm sorry," I said.

"Me too," Carina said. "You deserved to win."

"Brock Sances?" Mr. Hudson called his name through the bullhorn. Everyone searched the crowd for him. Once it was clear Brock wasn't there, Mr. Hudson called out the winners for Fourteens & Fifteens and Sixteens & Seventeens, along with the overall winner for upper grades.

"Because we had so many outstanding inventions this year, we added two new awards." Mr. Hudson held up a nine-inch stone carving of someone holding a large bowl over his head that was probably meant to represent our valley. "One goes to the overall winner for kids, and one to the overall winner for adults. For kids, this award goes to Aaren Grenwood for his medicine thermometer."

I screamed and jumped up and down along with Carina and Brenna. Aaren looked stunned, relieved, and thrilled all at the same time. He was in such a daze, he barely managed to give me Brenna's hand before he stumbled to the front to collect his award. The crowd hollered their appreciation of Aaren's invention as he walked back to us, his grin bigger than any I'd seen.

When Mr. Hudson was almost through announcing the winners in all the categories for adults, I heard a *psst*.

I looked at Carina. "They're starting the Twister after this," she said. "If we leave now, we can be first in line."

"Wanna get in line?" I asked Aaren. He gave me a look

like he couldn't believe I'd suggest something as wrong as missing out on science-related awards, so I sighed and shook my head no.

"This was a great year for inventions." Mr. Hudson put his hand on the six-foot-high stone obelisk that sat in the middle of the platform. "Within the next week, everyone who has won today will have their names carved into the Difference of One stone. Congratulations, winners!"

Aaren's name would be carved for the fourth time—twice as a grade-level winner, once as a middle-grade winner, and now once as an overall winner. When Aaren looked like he'd finished basking in his win enough to leave, Carina and I pulled him and Brenna to the Twister. There was way too much fun to be had to spend any more time on inventions.

Apparently Carina wasn't the only one with the idea to get to the Twister early. Lots of kids beat us to the line next to the twelve-foot circle of wood, raised by a rod in the middle, with a three-foot wall around the outside. Ten kids sat inside at a time, their backs against the wall, while the older kids and adults spun the circle as fast as they could. Trying to stay standing when you got off the ride was almost as much fun as the way the spinning sucked you to the wall during the ride.

"Puppy!" Brenna squealed as Holden Newberry got in line behind us, cradling his dog.

Holden put his dog on the ground, and Aaren let go of Brenna's hand as she bent down to pet him.

"I'm gonna lift my butt when they first start spinning," Holden said. "Then when it gets going fast, I'm gonna lift my legs to see if the force will hold me off the ground like I'm floating!"

"We have to try it," I said to Aaren and Carina as we moved forward in the line. "We'll see who can stay up the longest."

I could almost feel my guts being pulled backward as I watched the kids on the Twister go around and around. If only there weren't so many ahead of us in line. The performances might start before we got a second turn.

"Brenna, do you—" I was going to ask if she wanted to sit between Aaren and me, but when I turned around, she was gone.

Great Seats

11

"Brenna?" Aaren called out, his voice panicked.

"My dog!" Holden said. "He's gone, too!"

The four of us left the line and searched for Brenna. The crowds were so thick, I couldn't see her at all. Aaren and I ran to the solar ovens, to the inventions tables, then to the obelisk. Nothing. We were about to leave to search by the horses when Aaren froze. "The river!"

We rushed all the way to the bank, hoping to see the kids she'd begged to play with, but the bank was empty. Aaren ran left, toward the mill, but something about the path to my right made me take that direction. I didn't think she'd go past the clump of trees at the edge of the river since it was a natural boundary, but I went past them anyway, calling her name every step of the way. A few hundred feet down the path, I finally saw her, walking toward me with Holden's puppy in her arms. Two men I'd never seen before walked close behind her.

"Hope!" Brenna called as she walked to me. Seeing her by the men sent a chill up my spine, but she had a smile on her face, so I guessed everything was okay.

"Your friend got a little lost," the taller man said.

It was a strange thing for him to say, since Brenna knew all of White Rock and he obviously didn't know his way around at all. There wasn't any part of the Harvest Festival near the lake, but that was the direction they'd come from.

I grabbed Brenna's hand. "Are *you* lost?" I asked the man.

He smiled, and his voice came out smooth and confident. "Not at all. We were just admiring your beautiful valley."

The leathery look of his skin made it hard to guess if he was thirty or fifty. His sun-bleached light brown hair was wavy on top and brushed away from his forehead. The most noticeable thing about him, though, was a scar that ran from his right temple down to his jaw. Both men were thin and muscled, their clothes well worn but clean. The second man was shorter and had darker hair and skin.

He smiled, too. I was positive I hadn't seen either of them when we greeted the people from Browning at the tunnel yesterday.

"Where are you from?" I asked.

The taller man gestured over the river. "A little town called Bergen, about eighty miles south of here." He paused for a moment while I stared at him, then he added, "The name's Mickelson. We came to talk with your city about possible trade."

I'd heard about Bergen. Sometimes a group left White Rock to trade with another town, or to search for things left behind from before the bombs. They always stayed in Bergen when they traveled in that direction. And sometimes people from Bergen stopped in White Rock to bring news or to offer trades.

"Looks like we came at just the right time, too," the man said. "This is quite the celebration." He walked past me around the clump of trees and looked toward the festivities. "And it looks like you're about to miss out on some kind of performance." Both men walked toward the crowd.

"The Showdown," Brenna said. "We have to see it!"

We rounded the trees as Aaren ran toward us.

"Brenna! You were supposed to stay by me!"

Brenna glanced at the dog in her arms. "But the puppy ran away. Those men helped me catch her."

Aaren scooped up the puppy in one arm and held

Brenna's hand with the other. I looked to the crowd that had gathered around the performance platform, and Aaren followed my gaze. "We'll watch the Showdown. Just don't let go of my hand."

The Showdown was a Harvest Festival tradition. The Sixteens & Seventeens always did a difficult dance that got better every year. The teachers usually did a funny skit that made everyone laugh. Then the winning performance was chosen by the crowd.

We found Carina and Holden and gave Holden his puppy back before we all joined the rest of the audience at the performance platform. Just like the Twister line, though, we got there too late. The whole town had already found a place to watch. We walked around the circle, but the backs of all the adults who stood blocked our view.

If we were higher, we could see. The mill was only a dozen feet away from the edge of the crowd, and it had a section of flat roof with angled sides leading to it. "See those crates?" I asked the others. "If we pushed them a bit, we could use them as stairs to climb on that roof to watch."

Carina and Holden ran straight for them. Aaren paused a moment, then shook his head. "No, I don't want Brenna up there. You go. We'll stay down here."

Brenna huffed. "But I wanna go with Hope!"

"We'll find a good spot." Aaren led her through the

crowd, and they wiggled their way in. I ran to the crates and climbed up just behind Carina and Holden. The angled part of the roof was barely over a foot wide, and my right shoulder and hip rubbed against the building wall as I crawled, so it took a little balance. I moved carefully past a sharp metal piece of the roof that stuck up, and before I even got to the flat part, I could see the performance platform. This was a great spot.

It wasn't long before Ellie and Paige joined us. Nate climbed the other side of the roof and sat down next to Holden. A minute later, Brock climbed up, looking like he was carrying a million worries.

Nate slapped him on the back. "Congrats on winning the Inventions Contest!"

Brock smiled bigger than I'd seen him smile in a long time. "I won?"

"Yes!" I said. "Where were you?"

The smile left his face for a moment. "Busy." He looked toward the platform. "These are great seats!"

I glanced at the seven of us sitting on the roof and chuckled. Maybe my dad was right—people followed me more than I realized. Or at least they did when it meant great seats for the Showdown.

The kids in Sixteens & Seventeens did flips off each other's shoulders, spun on the platform, and leapt over one another, all while two of them stomped rhythmically on the floor of the platform.

I watched in a trance until I heard Aaren's worried shout from below: "Brenna!"

My eyes found Aaren. He was turning around, searching for Brenna as he worked his way through the crowd. I searched, too. I figured I'd find her first, since I had the better vantage point, but I couldn't see her at all.

I heard a scraping sound to my left, and I knew even before I saw Aaren look up in alarm that Brenna was climbing onto the roof. Aaren ran to the crates as I climbed over Ellie and Paige to get to Brenna. The roof was too narrow, and she wasn't good at balancing. I panicked when I saw her. She wasn't even crawling—she was trying to walk up the incline. I reached the angled part of the roof just as Aaren got both knees up onto it, Brenna teetering between us.

Then she lost her balance. She swung her arms around in circles, trying to stay upright, but she couldn't. I reached to grab her as Aaren stumbled forward. I somehow managed to catch one of her arms and hold her steady. I let out a huge breath of relief.

Then I looked behind Brenna.

Aaren's foot slipped as he lurched for Brenna. He fell to the roof on his stomach and tumbled off the edge. I heard the tear of fabric as he fell, and I knew he'd been cut from the piece of metal roofing that stuck up.

"Aaren!" I screamed as I looked over the edge.

For a moment, I couldn't move. It felt like a hand reached inside my chest and squeezed the life out of my heart. Aaren had landed on his back, crushing a wooden crate, his shirt covered in blood.

Consequences

I shouted for help as I lowered Brenna to a crate, then I jumped off the roof and knelt by Aaren. His face was white and scrunched up in pain.

"Please be okay, Aaren." I held his hand and hovered my other hand over the cut that went all the way across his stomach. I didn't know if I should press on it with my hand, or if that would make it worse. "Please, Aaren. Please be okay."

A crowd instantly gathered around us. Dr. Grenwood pushed her way through it.

"Ellie," Dr. Grenwood said. "Grab my medical bag. It's by the ovens. Brock, get some tablecloths." She nodded in the direction of two boys from Sixteens & Seventeens. "I need my stretcher from my office. Take two horses and ride down. Fast! Cass Williams!" she called loudly. When Cass slid into the front of the crowd, Dr. Grenwood said, "Get a wagon ready." Cass turned and ran toward the horses as Dr. Grenwood carefully lifted up Aaren's shirt. "Aaren. Sweetie, look at me."

His eyes fluttered open, and he squinted toward his mom.

"I know it hurts, but I need you to stay awake and keep your breathing steady. Can you do that for me?"

Aaren nodded. His dad reached us, hunched down across from me, and held Aaren's other hand tightly in his. When Ellie and Brock returned with the medical bag and tablecloths, I helped Aaren's dad fold one to put under his legs and another for under his head. My hands shook as we laid one over his legs to keep him warm. Brenna just stared at him, tears rolling down her face.

Dr. Grenwood dabbed disinfectant on Aaren's stomach, which made Aaren gasp and grind his teeth, then his eyes drifted closed. I wanted to do something to help, but I didn't have a clue in the world what to do. My hands and my stomach quivered—I wasn't sure if it was from the guilt or the worry or the helplessness, or all three.

Nothing felt real. Like I watched from a distance, only picking up on things that didn't matter. Like how Aaren's mom's hair was just as wavy as his. Or how her hands never stopped moving. Or how Aaren's eyelashes were so light, they were almost invisible. Then Dr. Grenwood spoke, pulling me back to the moment, my emotions crashing inside me.

"Stay with me, Aaren." Dr. Grenwood rubbed a cream on the wound to numb the pain. "Aaren, look at me. I need your help."

Aaren sucked in a breath and opened his eyes.

Dr. Grenwood kept glancing at Aaren's face as she worked. "Son, I have a patient who is injured and going into shock. What do you do to treat shock?"

Aaren's eyes focused, and his voice came out scratchy and slurred. "Um. Keep him awake and breathing normally. Keep him warm. And . . ." His brow furrowed in concentration. "Elevate his legs."

"Very good."

I squeezed Aaren's hand again. "I'm sorry, Aaren. I shouldn't have gone up! I knew Brenna wanted to follow me. I'm sorry. I'm so sorry."

Aaren's dad reached out and placed his hand on my arm. "It'll be okay," he whispered. I looked into his eyes, and they showed uncertainty. Then the doubt left, and in a commanding voice, he said, "It'll be okay." Like if he believed it strongly enough, it'd be true. He wrapped his arm around Brenna to calm her trembling. "It'll be okay."

Dr. Grenwood took an instrument from her bag and

gently prodded the wound with it. "This patient has a stomach wound. What would I do?"

Aaren took a few breaths. "Disinfect it. See if any internal organs were cut."

"The wound is deep, but the organs look okay. Hm. The small intestine may be cut." Dr. Grenwood packed the wound with gauze. "What's next?"

Aaren groaned. "Um. Stitch it closed and give the patient an antibiotic." Then Aaren started breathing too fast. "But the Ameiphus isn't ready. It won't be ready for weeks!"

I glanced up when Aaren's dad stiffened at his panic, and saw the curly-haired man from the river right behind him. The man disappeared into the crowd just as quickly as my eyes flew back to Aaren.

Dr. Grenwood gave Aaren's arm a pat. "It's okay, Aaren. We have one dose left from last year's batch. You're doing great. Just a few more minutes and we'll get you to my office."

I felt a hand on my shoulder and looked up to see my dad. He gave me a sad smile, but the worried look on his face made my stomach churn, so I looked back to Aaren. He fought to keep his eyes open, but he couldn't. I wished over and over that I could turn back time. Make it not happen. I couldn't believe I'd cared so much about being able to see the Showdown. It all seemed so stupid now.

When the two boys returned with the stretcher, Dr. Grenwood pulled strips of fabric from her medical bag and wrapped Aaren's cut tightly. "Son, we're going to move you now." Aaren didn't even open his eyes or nod. His parents, along with the two kids from Sixteens & Seventeens, moved Aaren onto the stretcher, then carried him to the wagon. I ran alongside the stretcher, hoping Dr. Grenwood would ask me to ride in the wagon with them. I wanted to be with Aaren. To know that everything was going to be okay. But no one asked me to, and I couldn't get my voice to work. Mr. Grenwood told Aaren's older sister Thalie to watch Brenna before climbing onto the wagon himself.

Then they left.

I stood at the edge of the road, unable to move as I watched the wagon disappear behind the trees long before it traveled the mile and a half down to City Circle. I'm not sure how long I stayed there, staring at the empty road, wishing that what had happened to my best friend was a mistake. A dream. Not real.

But I knew that only something real could make my heart hurt so much.

13
Goodbye

A snowflake landed on my nose and I pulled my winter coat around me tighter. It amazed me that it had turned so cold when the Harvest Festival was only three weeks ago. My parents and I, along with a hundred others, stood at the opening to the tunnel to say goodbye to our guard.

We didn't need our guard during the winter. With the Bomb's Breath protecting any entrance from over the mountain, the tunnel was the only way into White Rock. The windstorms on the plains blew the heavy snows into the tunnel and completely blocked it, so we didn't have to fear bandit attacks. Browning wasn't so lucky. They lived ten miles past White Rock, on the flat plains. Their city walls and their own guard weren't enough to protect them. Bandits didn't farm, so when they got hungry, they attacked towns for food.

I heard snow crunch behind me and turned to see Aaren, in actual sunlight for the first time since the Harvest Festival.

"Do you think there'll be enough snow to build a fort?" he asked.

I grinned. His voice was still weak, but at least he had enough energy to stand up—I hadn't seen that since before the accident. It made my heart feel lighter than it had in weeks. "There's no way your mom will give you permission."

His parents had let me see him the night he was injured, but he wasn't awake. It wasn't until a couple of days later that I actually saw him with his eyes open. The first two weeks after his injury, he could barely move. Every free moment I had, I sat on the edge of his bed, told him about school, and read him chapters from our science book. He was too exhausted to even hold the book himself. I was surprised he was able to come today.

He shook his head. "There may have to be sneaking involved."

He was teasing, of course, or he wouldn't have said it with my parents right next to us. Besides, there was no way he could build a fort. He probably couldn't even make a snowball—there was still a fear the wound would reopen with any movement.

"I'm glad you got to come see your brothers off," I said. "I didn't think your mom would let you out of bed."

"I had to say goodbye." He bit his lip and looked to where his brothers, Travin and Cole, tightened tarps over a wagon.

"You're going to miss them."

He nodded.

I was going to miss them, too. They'd lived next to me all my life. They'd teased me and protected me almost as much as I guessed real brothers would.

We watched the preparations in silence. This year we had more guards going to Browning to help than ever before. When the people from Browning had traveled home from the Harvest Festival, they were attacked, and the bandits took the food and supplies we'd traded with them. When we got word, panic spread through White Rock. Things were getting worse and everyone felt it. Several people from White Rock volunteered to be guards as their splits through the winter, so the number of guards going grew from eighteen to thirty.

Thirty guards, and they probably wouldn't all make it back home.

My dad told me that anyone who was a bandit could live in a town instead—there were more than enough towns that took in strangers—but they were the ones who didn't want the responsibility or the work that came with joining a settlement. They just wanted to take what they needed. Before the bombs, there was a central government. Kind of like we have now in White Rock, but it was everywhere—even in areas where there were no towns, like on the plains where the bandits roamed. He said there were police officers, which I thought must be kind of like guards, and they'd stop people from stealing. But since we didn't have any police or guards on the plains, there was no one to stop the bandits.

Aaren's mom was loading medical supplies into a wagon when my mom noticed a tear run down her cheek. This was the first year her two oldest sons were joining the guard. "I'll be right back," my mom said, then rushed to Dr. Grenwood.

While they made last-minute checks on the wagons, I kicked at the ground. The snow was packed hard here, about ten inches deep, but with the strong winds on the plains, the guards said the drifts were more than three feet high at the other end of the tunnel. With the snowstorm that was just starting and the strong winds expected to follow it, they figured the snow would be over six feet high—and completely impassable—in just two days' time. It seemed the spring and summer rain we should have gotten earlier had decided to all come now.

I looked toward the tunnel and noticed Brock standing by himself in the crowd, watching the guards work. It took me a while to figure out what was different about his facial expressions. Everyone else was sad the guard members were leaving, but Brock looked like he wanted to join them.

Stott, the Captain of the Away Guard, walked up to my dad. "Are you sure we can't take any more guns?"

My dad looked to the east, as if he could see through the mountains, and shook his head. "If we're going to keep sending this many guards to Browning, we'll have to make a trek to the gunsmith at Wilson's Hollow before long. No town has been willing to trade for guns at any price lately. Is everything loaded?" Stott nodded, and my dad turned to me. "Time to say goodbye."

As I walked toward the guard members, I saw Mr. Williams from the mines tie down a tarp that covered an open-topped wagon. He looked terrible. His eyes were red and puffy, his face was blotchy, and he focused on the knots like he was trying to turn off the world. But the strangest thing was that his dog Sandy wasn't at his heels. Something was definitely wrong.

"Dad?" I called out. "Where's Sandy?"

He took a breath, then exhaled. "Ken was walking her along the road at the top of the woods on the fourth ring.

A squirrel ran across their path and Sandy chased it past the warning fences."

"Did Sandy go into the Bomb's Breath?"

He rubbed his hand over his face.

"Sandy's dead?" Aaren asked.

When my dad bowed his head, I knew the answer was yes. I felt sick.

"We're crazy to live so close to something so dangerous," he muttered. Almost like he was saying it to himself. "Come on. They're leaving soon."

I followed him, numb. Sandy was dead. Mr. Williams didn't look right without Sandy by his side. Nothing was right with this day.

Just like every year, I was saying goodbye to people I'd known my whole life. It was worse this year, though—it was the first time I had to say goodbye to Aaren's brothers. It seemed wrong to send them into such great danger, while we sat in our safe, protected valley. We ran out of Ameiphus when Aaren got hurt, so we couldn't even send some with the guard to treat injuries.

I stood next to Aaren while his siblings hugged Travin and Cole; then it was our turn. I told them I'd miss them and to be safe, and they hugged me like I was one of their sisters. Cole rubbed his knuckles through Aaren's hair and said, "You're the oldest son at home now. Watch out for everyone, okay?" Aaren told him that he would, then looked away.

When his mom began to cry the moment she put her arms around Travin, and my mom started crying about half a second later, I helped Aaren walk back to a wagon. He didn't say a word. Neither did I. What was I supposed to say to him? Eventually I managed, "They'll be okay. They'll be back." I wasn't sure how convincing I sounded.

14

News

All of us at the council meeting fidgeted as we listened to Mr. Williams talk about the amount of coal mined for the winter, and Ray Romanek talk about the amount of firewood we had. I didn't blame us for being antsy. Today marked the fourth week since the guard left. Every Wednesday at four p.m., someone from White Rock went to our side of the pass and someone from Browning went to their side of the pass, and they communicated with the telegraph system that Mr. Hudson had made.

It was almost five, time for the meeting to end, and everyone drummed their fingers, wiggled in their seats, and looked to the doors almost constantly, barely listening to the speaker. People filled all the empty spots in the room. We all wanted news on whether Browning had been attacked, and if so, how our guard fared.

Brock joined Aaren and me at our normal spot against the far wall, and Brenna sat on her mom's lap on the benches.

Finally, when virtually everyone was staring at the double doors at the side of the gym instead of paying attention to the speaker, Joey Kearney burst through them and ran up onto the platform at the front. Out of breath and panting, he said, "They're fine. There have been *no* attacks."

We all let out a relieved breath. My mom and Aaren's mom, who both sat on the front row of benches, hugged each other. Even Brock sighed in relief. I turned to Aaren and grinned.

Mrs. Beckinwood got up from the council head's seat, walked to Joey, and patted him on the shoulder. "That is good news, Joey. Good news." Mrs. Beckinwood's eyes went to the side doors for a moment, as if she'd heard something. Then she turned back to Joey. "Before we know it, winter will be over and we'll have our boys back home where they'll—"

Then everyone's attention flew to the doors as we heard a rumbling. Kind of like thunder, but much closer. Like it was happening right outside the room.

About as quickly as the sound started, it stopped. We all turned to look at the person next to us with confused faces just as the doors at the front, back, and sides of the gym burst open. Men filed into the room, dressed in dirty coats and snow-covered boots. Men I'd never seen before. Men with guns aimed at us. Mrs. Beckinwood froze with her hand still on Joey's shoulder.

One of the men yelled, "Nobody move!"

I didn't. I couldn't. I stood like a statue in a shocked stupor. There were people we didn't know in White Rock. During winter. When we were isolated. Safe.

The men spread out along the aisles at the side, front, and back of the room, surrounding us and blocking all the exits. My heart clenched tight, and every beat hurt. My breath came fast and a cold sweat covered my arms and back, making goose bumps everywhere. I couldn't think.

The side doors opened again, and two men entered who I *did* recognize. The tall, curly-haired man with the scar that I'd seen near the river at the Harvest Festival—Mickelson—and his shorter, darker-skinned friend. They both strode to the front of the room. The shorter man stopped as they neared the platform, but Mickelson stepped onto the platform, next to where Mrs. Beckinwood and Joey still stood.

I held my breath as Mickelson stared down the entire gym. "Your town has something we want." He pulled a gun from his hip—one that looked like it had been made before the bombs—and waved it carelessly as he walked around the table, stopping for a moment behind each council member. "So, tell me. Who's in charge?"

"He's going to hurt Mrs. Beckinwood," Brock whispered. "I can see it in his eyes."

My dad could see it, too. I watched with horror as his focus shifted from Mickelson to where Joey's support was all that kept Mrs. Beckinwood from collapsing on unsteady knees. Then my dad looked to my mother, seated in the front row. He mouthed one word. *Sorry.*

My mom's hands flew to her mouth and she shook her head in panic.

"No," I said, though my voice came out a whisper.

The sound of my dad's chair legs scraping across the wooden platform silenced every murmur. He stood tall and drew in a breath. "I am."

The man raised his gun slightly and shot my dad in the thigh.

"No!" I screamed as everyone in the room rose to their feet. We were standing so far from my dad. I tried to run toward him but couldn't seem to move. It took a moment before I realized Brock and Aaren were holding my torso.

Aaren whispered a frantic "Don't go."

The words didn't make sense. Every part of me wanted to run to my dad.

"Stay, Hope. Please." Aaren's voice was urgent in my

ear. "My mom's already to him. See? She'll help him. Stay, please."

The room blurred in some places and shone abnormally clear in others. The walls closed in. I couldn't suck in enough air.

Mickelson aimed his gun toward the crowd. "Sit down," he commanded as Dr. Grenwood packed my dad's wound with gauze to stop the bleeding. The man meandered to the front of the platform, totally at ease. "You're a trusting town. I need you to trust that our guns *do* have bullets, and that we aren't afraid to use them."

"We . . . we have food stores," Mr. Sances stammered from his seat on the platform. "We're willing to share everything we can."

The man raised an eyebrow. "That's not what we came for. We want your antibiotics."

Whispers filled the room.

Mr. Sances glanced at Mrs. Beckinwood as Joey helped her to a chair, then at my dad, who lay on the platform, wincing as Dr. Grenwood pressed on his leg. "Our Ameiphus? It didn't grow well this year, and our latest batch isn't finished. But we can offer you food or other supplies."

Mickelson's voice was calm and controlled, yet somehow filled every inch of the gym. "You don't know the value of Ameiphus, or how rare it is, if you're offering food and supplies in its place."

Mr. Sances looked around, as if searching for confirmation that he was hearing right, or answering right. "Is someone hurt? Does someone have Shadel's? Tell your men to put down their guns and we'll talk about getting you help. Maybe when the new medicine is finished, we can give you a few doses of Ameiphus."

The scarred man ignored Mr. Sances and walked straight to my dad's side. I wanted to scream at him to stay away from my dad, but my mouth wouldn't work. My lungs wouldn't work. Aaren and Brock still held on to me, even though my legs wouldn't work.

Mickelson crouched down across from Dr. Grenwood and said, "No. I want it all."

My dad suddenly looked like he was in a lot more pain, and Dr. Grenwood scowled. She met Mickelson's eyes and said, "It's not ready."

Mickelson stood up. "Explain."

"It takes weeks to turn the mold from Ameiphus into an antibiotic in a usable form," Dr. Grenwood said. "It's not finished yet."

Mickelson waved his gun in the general direction of everyone seated in the gym. "So tell me, Doctor. How long will me and my men be the guests of the good people of White Rock while we wait for the antibiotics to be ready?"

Aaren's mom stopped working on my dad's leg and bit her lower lip. "It's in the refining and purifying stage. If I could get enough stabilizers and bulkers in powder form to press the medicine into tablets, I might be able to finish in three days."

Mickelson narrowed his eyes at Dr. Grenwood, like he was trying to guess if she was overestimating. "You have until sundown two days from now. I suggest you get him patched up quickly, because if you don't meet the deadline, you'll need to worry less about finding that bullet and more about finding coffins."

The Lineup

The smell of vegetable soup and baking bread wafted from the kitchen. Aaren and Brenna sat beside me on the wooden bench where my mom usually sat for town meetings. I rocked back and forth with my arms wrapped around my knees and waited for news of my dad. My fingers were numb from the cold, but I couldn't seem to make myself move—even to get closer to the hearth fires.

Before Mickelson let Dr. Grenwood have men carry my dad down the hall to the clinic, he demanded the town's records so they could make a list of everyone age fourteen and over. In the last two hours, Mickelson's men had gathered anyone who'd stayed home from the council meeting and brought them to the community center to be counted.

Now every member of White Rock huddled in the gym or in one of the classrooms. The bandits even put people in the library. This building was designed to house everyone in White Rock in an emergency, but we didn't have much space. With bandits in every room, at least it meant there were only six in the gym with us, instead of thirty-four.

"Is it supposed to take this long?" I asked Aaren for easily the twelfth time as his dad walked toward us.

Mr. Grenwood put his hand on my shoulder to stop my rocking and answered for Aaren. "Yes, it's normal. My wife's good at this kind of thing, Hope. She'll be done soon. Your mom will be in here the second that bullet comes out to let you know how he's doing. And if you need anything, we're just right over there." Mr. Grenwood pointed to the rest of Aaren's family, gathered near one of the hearth fires; then he took Brenna's hand and led her back to them.

When Joey and Dr. Grenwood came through the door supporting my dad, I leapt up and helped them position him with his back against the wall. My mom sat next to him and held his hand with both of hers.

I knelt down, wrapped my arms around his neck, and gave him the tightest hug I dared. "Are you okay?"

"I'll be all right, pumpkin. Are *you* okay? Things got a little scary in here." His voice sounded so strained, like even talking hurt.

I nodded and wiped away a stray tear, then turned to Dr. Grenwood. "Shouldn't he be in a bed at the clinic?"

Dr. Grenwood tucked a curl behind her ear as she adjusted the bandage on his leg. "Yes, he should. But your dad's tough."

"We had our own personal bandit watching us in there"—my dad's eyes searched the room as Mr. Newberry wandered toward us, trying not to be noticed by the bandits—"and I need to talk with the council. Is Newberry the only one here?"

"Yeah," I said. "They split up the council—one to a room."

He grunted, then squeezed my mom's and my hands. "Can you two give us a minute?"

Aaren, my mom, and I scooted a few feet away but stayed close enough to hear their whispered conversation.

My dad coughed a couple of times. It was like the cough emptied his entire body of air. He took a deep breath, then said in a voice that sounded like it took more energy than he had, "Any word on how the bandits got in? Joey would've seen them if they came through the pass."

"Nope. Not through the pass," Mr. Newberry said. "Burke Davies was at the ball mill when the bandits collected everyone who wasn't at the meeting. He said bandits were guarding the mines."

The mines! My mind flashed to the hole in the mine floor Mr. Williams had shown us on our field trip, then to the Harvest Festival when I saw Mickelson and the shorter man on the path by the river. I felt sick.

My dad exhaled like he was in a lot of pain. "I thought there wasn't a way in or out through those caves!"

Mr. Newberry shrugged. "I guess we were wrong."

His words sent chills down my back, because it was so close to what Mr. Allen had said when he talked about the choices made in World War III. I suppose, in a way, I was witnessing White Rock's history being made.

Mr. Newberry took a breath like he was going to say something else, but the nine p.m. whistle blew, the doors at the back of the gym burst open, and Mickelson strolled in.

"Line up!"

My mom jumped to her feet. Panic filled her face as she glanced between the line forming and my dad, probably because she hated to leave him while she lined up.

In the moment she hesitated, a dark-haired bandit came over and yelled, "You heard the man. He said, 'Line up!'" Then he shoved her really hard, knocking her to the floor with enough force that she skidded several feet.

People ran forward, grabbed her, and pulled her into the line.

"Get in line!" the same bandit yelled, and I turned

from my mom just in time to see it was my dad he yelled at. *My dad.* He didn't look like he could move an inch, let alone line up.

It was too much. I couldn't sit and do nothing while he treated my parents that way. Without thinking, I stepped between the bandit and my dad. "He can't!" I yelled. "You guys shot him!"

I saw a blur of motion from the bandit's arm, but he was so quick. There wasn't any time to duck or turn as his open hand hit my face and sent me sprawling to the floor. My hand flew to the stinging pain in my cheek.

"*Everyone* over fourteen lines up. Everyone *under* fourteen stays out of the way and doesn't make problems for everyone else."

I wasn't too injured to catch the threat in his voice—he'd punish everyone if I didn't keep my mouth shut. A couple of my neighbors helped my dad while I moved away from the line. Aaren and Carina joined me, not saying a word, and Brenna buried her face against Aaren.

Mickelson and the six bandits went up and down the line and smacked people who didn't stand straight enough, or who made the line crooked, or who muttered something under their breath. Anything they could do to make people more afraid.

The looks on the faces of everyone in my town made my heart sink into my stomach. They were so afraid and already giving up hope. It wouldn't take long before every one of them would hand over the Ameiphus to get the bandits to leave.

The sharp pain in my cheek slowly changed to a burning heat, and I could tell the handprint was starting to swell. But that didn't stop me from worrying about my parents. They needed help. The entire town needed help. There was nothing any of us could do to stop the bandits. Not without weapons and not without our guard. We had neither.

Even if the bandits didn't shoot anyone else, without our medicine, people would die. Someone had to find a way to get our guard!

Suddenly I realized that Mr. Hudson's mantra of "work with your strengths" could actually apply to me. So many times I'd thought about the things I'd willingly trade for being good at inventing. But for the first time ever, I thought about what I *wasn't* willing to trade. I definitely wouldn't trade my physical abilities. Maybe the fact that I always took too many risks could be a strength.

A fire burned in my chest as strong as the fire shaped like a bandit's hand on my cheek. Maybe *I* could get our guard.

Help

I went through everything in my head. I could escape through the loose paneling Aaren and I had found that led into the closed-off hallway. And I could go through the Bomb's Breath and over the mountain to get to Browning. I didn't exactly know where Browning was, except that it was northeast of us—the direction of the rock formation at the top of the mountain that looked like a shovel. If I started on the path we took to our cliff, I could continue on, keeping the Shovel in sight. When I reached the crest of the mountain, I'd be able to look down and see Browning on the plains. It was an entire town with almost as many people as White Rock, so it couldn't be hard to find.

The more I thought about it, the more I decided it

might be possible. It wouldn't be like sneaking off to sky jump, though. It could take a while. And if I went without telling my parents, they'd panic. But telling them would mean I'd have to confess to my dad that I'd jumped into the Bomb's Breath. I think every time he even heard the words *Bomb's Breath,* he thought of his childhood friends who'd died. If I told, he'd be so horrified, sky jumping would be over for me forever.

Losing the Bomb's Breath wasn't the biggest reason not to go, but the other reasons were too painful to think about.

Moment by moment, my dad looked worse. His face twisted in pain, and his skin was so pale, it was white. I knew he could pass out at any minute. The bandits had everyone counted, but still they harassed people and made them all stay in line. Maybe they did it to scare us. Maybe they did it to punish the town because of my outburst. Or maybe they did it to make my dad stand there longer.

Whatever their reason, it convinced me I'd made the right choice.

"I have to get them," I muttered.

Aaren's eyes bored into me, probably trying to figure out what I meant. I turned to him. "Aaren, I'm going to Browning to get our guard." I stuck my hands in my pockets to keep them from shaking as both Carina's and Aaren's eyes widened and Brenna looked at me in confusion. "I can sneak out. They only count fourteens and older, so they wouldn't miss me. You heard my dad and Mr. Newberry. They've got men guarding the mines, so no one could go for help that way. The only way to get help is by going through the Bomb's Breath and over the mountain. You know as well as I do that no one else would even consider it."

Aaren shook his head. "No, Hope. You can't go. You—What about your parents?"

My mom stood in the line with her shoulders hunched, her trembling arms hugging her torso. I pictured my dad's big, strong arms wrapped around her, protecting her from all harm like he always did. When I looked to my dad, though, he seemed anything but big and strong and capable of protecting her.

"I've helped my mom treat gunshot wounds before," Aaren said. "Bandits make their own bullets. They aren't sterile, and they aren't made of good metal like the ones we have. They break apart more. They cause bad infections."

I shook my head while he talked. This was the part I couldn't face. The thoughts I didn't want to have or they'd overwhelm me. Make me not want to go. I wished he'd stop, but he didn't.

"You think he looks bad now? This is the beginning,

Hope! He *will* get worse and worse, and without any Amei-phus he could die, and you wouldn't be here."

Brenna looked up with horror on her face. "Hope's dad is going to die?"

It was obvious Aaren had forgotten that Brenna was with us. "Oh, sorry, no. He'll be fine. Um . . ." He looked around until he spotted his thirteen-year-old sister, Beth, standing next to his ten-year-old sister, Lily. "Beth is right over there. See? Will you go to her for a few minutes?"

Brenna looked up at me with worry in her eyes, then ran to her sisters.

As soon as Brenna was out of hearing range, I whis-pered, "I know." I could barely breathe. "But don't you see? That's why I have to go! If I can get to Browning and bring back the guard members to save us, we can give him Ameiphus!"

Carina looked at Aaren and me, then grabbed my shoulders. "Hope, listen. It'd be crazy to go! And what about your mom? If your dad's going to get worse, can she handle that? She needs you!"

"But I might make it back in time. And if I don't go, he *will* die." I gestured to everyone in the line. "And what about them? Without the Ameiphus, a lot of them will die, too." I watched my dad as the people around him held him up. The lady next to my mom had an arm around her shoulders. "People here help each other," I whispered. "That's what I'm trying to do, too."

Aaren and I watched the line of those fourteen and older for a long time, seeing everyone flinch whenever a bandit walked past them. Carina just stared at me.

Finally, after what felt like an eternity, Aaren spoke. "You're right. There's not more than a couple of people up there who believe we can make it out of this without giving up the Ameiphus. We need our guard."

We all stood in silence as several bandits came in, one at a time, to report the count from each of their rooms.

"Do we tell your parents, or do we just sneak out?" Aaren asked.

My eyes went to his stomach. To where his shirt covered his injury. "Aaren . . . I don't want you to go."

He didn't say a word.

Going alone scared me more than I was willing to admit. I didn't know which was worse—trying to do something this big alone, or risking Aaren getting hurt more. Then I realized that it didn't matter. Aaren would find a way to join me. That was the kind of friend he was. He'd never leave me to do this alone.

"You're going to come anyway, aren't you?" I asked.

He grinned. "Yep."

I watched my mom's worried face as she looked past several people in the line to where my dad was being held in a standing position by those on either side of him. "Then yes," I said. "We tell."

"The numbers are in," Mickelson announced. "You're free to leave the line."

I let out a breath I'd been holding for too long and ran toward my parents.

The Only Option

My dad collapsed into the arms of the men beside him, and they carried him to the edge of the gym and propped him against the wall near a hearth. My mom rushed to his side. As soon as his arm was around her shoulder, her face relaxed a little. When I was four and both my mom's parents and my dad's dad all died within a few days of each other, my parents pulled each other through. They would get through this fine, too, even if I was gone.

Dr. Grenwood hurried into the room a few minutes later. While she took care of my dad, Aaren and I got soup and bread from the kitchen. My dad didn't want to eat, but with both Aaren's mom and my mom saying he should, and with me practically force-feeding him, he finally ate.

When he finished, he looked slightly better and was anxious to talk with Mr. Newberry again.

As Mr. Newberry ambled toward us, trying to act like he was just stretching his legs, Aaren, my mom, and I moved to the side so they could talk. I laid my head on my mom's shoulder.

Mr. Newberry sat down and, before my dad even said anything, suggested we attack the bandits. "We have the superior numbers," he said. "We could take them!"

"They have guns," my dad said in a strained voice. "And they'd shoot a lot of us in the process."

"What about *our* guns?" Mr. Newberry asked. "We can go to the cellar for food, distract the guard, and get to the weapons room. Even up the odds a bit."

"Since we sent so many men to Browning, we sent more guns. There are only two in the weapons room, along with a handful of bullets. It's not enough. We need to do something different."

"Just because you said you're in charge doesn't make it true," Mr. Newberry hissed. "And it doesn't mean you can make bad decisions for this town. I won't sit here while you roll over and let them take whatever they want."

My dad whispered, "Pull it together—getting angry isn't going to solve the problem. Neither is campaigning for council head." Then he coughed a few times and drew in a quick breath like the pain had gotten worse. After a moment of struggling to breathe normally, he said, "Right now, we're looking at solutions and their consequences. We need all options, and we need to think what the council members in the other rooms would vote to do."

One of the guards making rounds walked near enough to stop their conversation for a moment right as Dr. Grenwood came to check on my dad. But I still heard Mr. Newberry's angry breathing. It was probably a good thing he couldn't talk for a bit.

Brock walked over and stood awkwardly, then sat down next to me. After a moment of silence, he said, "I'm sorry about your dad. Is he okay?"

I shrugged. "For now."

The four of us sat in silence. When the guard wandered away, Mr. Newberry took a deep breath. "Fine. We'll guess what the others would do. Williams would give them all of the Ameiphus. Get them out as soon as possible."

At the suggestion, Dr. Grenwood exploded—in a whispered sort of way. "That's not an option! Do you know how many people would've died last year without Ameiphus? Over seventy. Seventy! If we give them the Ameiphus, it's the same as killing that many people!" She turned to my dad. "Please tell me you won't consider it. Reports from other towns say they stole food or weapons. Antibiotics can't be the only thing they want."

"It is." My dad sighed. "You know how rough life is out there. They get Shadel's Sickness just like we do. Probably more so, since they don't have good shelter. And I'm sure they get infections from injuries. They won't leave without it."

"Maybe if we offered *some* of the Ameiphus," Mr. Newberry said, "along with something else of value. We could reason with him."

"I don't know," my dad muttered. "Mickelson said we have no idea how valuable it is. They probably want it for trade, too, and they know they won't be able to catch us unprepared again. They'll want everything now."

The gym doors opened, and Mickelson strode into the room. Mr. Newberry lowered his voice and spoke quickly. "So, what? You're just going to let them take it? Fighting them is the only solution, and you know it, but you're too much of a coward to fight. This is why you should never be council head. You'd run this town into the ground!"

"Now that's—" Dr. Grenwood started to argue, but my dad cut her off and changed the subject to firewood for the hearths. Dr. Grenwood checked my dad's bandages.

Mickelson waved the dark-haired bandit over as he neared my dad and said, "We have two council members together." He jabbed Mr. Newberry's leg with his boot. "Get this one to the library." Mr. Newberry got up and threw my dad a look. I couldn't tell if it was a threat or a plea. Maybe it was both. He left the room with the bandit, and Mickelson turned to Aaren's mom. "Doctor, I believe you have some important work in the clinic that everyone's counting on you to do. And you have another patient."

I looked to my dad, then Mickelson, then Dr. Grenwood as she leapt to her feet.

Mickelson nodded in the general direction of the library. "Guy named Hudson. Said he was sick when my men picked him up. They stuck him in the library, and in the last few minutes, splotches appeared on his face— probably Shadel's. I don't care if you quarantine him in your office or kill him now to keep it from spreading, but if my men get sick before you finish the Ameiphus, your family's lives are forfeit."

"Go easy on that leg," Dr. Grenwood told my dad before she ran out of the room.

"No! Not Mr. Hudson," I whispered. He couldn't have Shadel's, especially when we had no Ameiphus. Our town needed Mr. Hudson.

When Mickelson finally sauntered away, Aaren and I moved closer to my dad. He had lines of worry and pain on his face, and it made him look a million years older.

"Dad, we need our guard."

"I know, pumpkin. But we'll make do." He closed his eyes and patted my hand.

I leaned closer and whispered, "Dad, I can get them."

His eyes flew open just as a guard walked near us. As he passed, I gulped down my fear, hopefully before my dad heard it in my voice. "There are bandits guarding the hole in the mines, and with the snowdrifts, no one can get through the tunnel. The *only* way to get to Browning right now is to go over the mountain. I've been through the Bomb's Breath, Dad. Both Aaren and I have. We can go through again and get our guard."

His face was already pale, but once I told him my secret, he looked worse. His breathing sped up and he clutched his chest. "Please tell me you didn't." His voice was a scratchy whisper.

Aaren flashed me a you're-harming-the-patient look, so I said what I thought he would say. "Take slow, deep breaths, Dad. I'm really sorry I didn't tell you before." I patted my shoulders twice. "But see? I'm fine, Dad. I'm fine. We've been going into the Bomb's Breath for two years, and we're fine."

I thought it would be better if he knew that it wasn't a onetime fluke, but when I mentioned the two years part, his breathing got faster and faster. I gave him a drink of water and bit my lip as I waited for his breathing to slow.

"Dad, you love this town. I know you'll do anything for it. But I know you don't want to fight or give away our Ameiphus, because lots of people will die. There's another option. You can let us get help."

My dad shook his head and looked behind me to my mom. "You're wrong, Hope. There are things I won't do for this town."

I spun around to my mom when I realized she had heard my confession, too. I expected her to look shocked or upset, but she didn't. She just got up from her spot next to Brock without saying a word, walked around to my dad's other side as he held out his hand toward her, and sat next to him. She gave me a look, but I couldn't figure out what it meant.

"And I definitely won't sacrifice my daughter for a chance at getting help." My dad reached out with his other hand and gently touched my swollen cheek. "I love this town a lot, Hope. But I love you and your mom even more."

"Mr. Toriella?" Aaren said. "We won't get caught. Honest."

"No," my dad said simply. "We'll find another option."

"Dad, there are no other options! We can do this." I glanced around to make sure I wasn't loud enough for a guard to hear, then whispered, "It's not too dangerous. I'm capable."

My dad let out a sound that at first I thought would be a chuckle, but ended up being chopped grunts of pain. "You're the most capable person I know, Hope." And then his voice became a strained whisper I could barely hear. "As a father, I would tell you no because of the deadliness of the Bomb's Breath alone. As the acting council head, I would tell any person—adult or child—no for a myriad of reasons. You're wrong, Hope. It *is* dangerous. There are a great number of things to fear. The risks are far too great."

I knew there was a lot to fear. The truth was, I was more scared than I'd been in my life. I was scared for my town, I was scared for Aaren and me, I was scared for my mom, and I was especially scared for my dad. I had to work to push all of that out of my mind and tell myself that if my dad were in my position, he'd go. I couldn't let my fear show on my face.

"Dad, this is the option that will save the town."

"No. Absolutely not," my dad said. "No chance. No to both of you. There's another option; we just need to find it."

My dad struggled to adjust the way he was sitting against the wall. He'd looked a little better after he ate, but now his face looked grayish. I reached out and touched his forehead—it was getting hot. That meant the infection had set in. The last teeny hope I'd had that he'd get better on his own was gone.

I looked into his eyes, so full of sadness and worry, and I could tell that he knew there was no other option. He was just protecting me, like he always protected everyone.

And if I didn't go, he would die.

18
Time to Go

That night was the longest of my life. Even counting the time I had the mottled cough and the constant coughing kept me awake. Just before we went to bed, Aaren's mom came to check on my dad and said that Melina Johnson, a little girl from Sixes & Sevens, was coming down with Shadel's Sickness. I'd lived through enough winters to know that two people getting sick so close to the same time usually meant the beginning of an outbreak. I kept thinking about how many people Dr. Grenwood said usually got the sickness each year, and how that could all happen in the next couple of weeks. Without the Ameiphus, they'd die. I stared out the high window, wishing the night sky would lighten so I could stop trying to fall asleep.

We had enough food stored in the community center to feed everyone for a few weeks, but we didn't have blankets. The hearth fires burned low, and the winter cold seeped through the walls. I shifted back and forth on the floor, trying to make a pillow out of my coat sleeves while covering as much of myself as I could with the rest. Every time my brain turned off enough to sleep, the hourly whistle blew, and everyone fourteen and older stumbled awake and into lines to be counted. I think the bandits did it to drive us insane. It was working.

I gave up sleeping after the four a.m. whistle and was tense and ready long before the five o'clock whistle blew. If Aaren and I left at five o'clock, the sun would be coming up about the time we crossed through the Bomb's Breath and into unfamiliar territory. We'd decided it would be best to climb the mountain in daylight.

I looked at the lumps of sleeping bodies strewn across the gym floor, and then at my parents, who slept with their heads near me. My dad's face was barely visible in the orange light from the coals in the hearth, but judging by his scrunched-up forehead covered with little beads of sweat, he was in pain and his fever was bad. Every minute that passed meant he was getting worse. I wanted to reach out and touch his face once before I left, but I was afraid I'd wake him.

My mom's head moved and drew my attention. She was watching me with a strange expression on her face.

"Mom? Why are you awake?"

She reached out and put her hand on mine. "When you were a baby, Hope," she whispered, "you crawled at an impossibly young age."

I had no idea why she was talking about crawling. Maybe she was sleep-talking.

"Before I knew it, you were this teeny little thing who could walk and get into all sorts of trouble." She paused for a moment, then squeezed my hand. "I stepped into the yard one day when you were not more than a year and a half. You'd climbed up that wooden fence by the coops and you had your arms out, balancing while you walked across the board at the top. My scream startled you, and you fell into a puddle on the ground. When I gathered your little mud-covered body up into my arms and held you tight, I knew." She gave me a small smile. "Right then I knew that someday you'd walk away to do something incredibly dangerous, and I'd have to let you go. That there were going to be things that no one else could do as well as you, and I'd have to let you do them."

A tear ran down my cheek, and she reached out and wiped it off with a hand that didn't shake even a little bit. I could barely see her in the darkness, but she didn't look fragile. I wondered what had happened between the nine p.m. lineup and now.

"Hope, I've seen you get yourself out of one pickle after another. You get yourself out of this one and come back, okay?"

I nodded. "I will."

She rose onto an elbow and reached for something by her side. "Here." She pushed a burlap sack toward me. "When I was cleaning up after dinner, I snuck food for your trip. Mr. Hudson has snowshoes in his shed for when he and his sons check the weather instruments. You should stop and get those."

She smiled, and I saw the fear she was hiding. I could tell she was trying to be stronger than she felt, like I was. More than anything, I wanted to tell her that everything would be fine—for me and for them. That she didn't need to worry. The words never came, so I just gave her a hug. "I love you, Mom."

"I love you, too." Her gaze followed mine to my dad's face. She picked up his hand and held it in hers. "Don't worry. I'll look out for him."

My dad had told me that when he and my mom were about to graduate from Sixteens & Seventeens, his mom died. She had been their math and English teacher. My mom was the one who'd helped him get through it. She'd wrapped her arms around him and whispered that every-thing would be okay. They'd spent hours together every day, and eventually he confessed that he'd liked her for the past twelve years. During the time when she'd had all the miscarriages, my dad had been the one to wrap his arms around her and whisper that everything would be okay. I guessed it was her turn again.

I kissed my dad's too-hot hand as the five a.m. whistle blew.

The guards roused themselves from their seats and yelled for everyone to line up as people groaned, mothers shushed their babies, and the adults shuffled to the line. My mom and Aaren's parents helped my dad get to his place in the line. In the midst of the mass of bodies stand-ing and stepping over the huddled lumps of sleeping kids in the dim light, I picked up the coat I'd been using as a blanket, slipped it on the right way, and grabbed my bag, pushing the burlap sack my mom had given me inside it. I waited for Aaren; then we snuck to our secret opening behind the paneling. I took one last look at my parents before I slid it open, tossed in my bag, and ducked into the hidden hallway. Aaren did the same and let the panel shut behind him.

And just like that, we were on our own.

The dusty hallway was pitch-black, so I ran my hand against the wall as I tiptoed. When I reached the end of the hall, I felt around for the hanging rope, then handed it to Aaren. "You first."

Aaren tried, but mostly grunted. "You don't realize how many stomach muscles it takes to climb a rope until you don't have them!"

I locked my hands together to give him a boost up, then let him stand on my shoulders to reach the opening in the ceiling. I climbed up the rope behind him and into the crawl space between the ceiling and the roof of the building. Bandits likely walked in the hall below us to turn in the counts for each room, so we barely let each hand and knee make a sound as we moved.

I made it halfway down the crawl space, then heard a grunt. I spun on my knees and squinted in the darkness.

Silence.

I convinced myself I was hearing things and almost continued on, when I heard the sound of fabric brushing across wood.

"Don't move," I whispered into Aaren's ear. Then slowly, cautiously, I crawled along the passage back toward the opening.

"Out is *that* direction."

I froze in place, stunned by the voice. "Brock? You have to go back!"

He crawled forward and nudged me ahead. "I'll get caught if I go back."

Frustration covered every inch of me. Brock was right—there wasn't much time before the chaos of the lineup would die down, then every sound would be heard. Brock had been so quiet last night when I told my dad my plan, I'd completely forgotten that he was sitting next to my mom the whole time.

"You can't come," I said. "It's too dangerous!"

"You need me."

I let out a little laugh. Of all the things he could have said to convince me to let him come, he chose *You need me*. What did he think I needed him for? Figuring out how to climb a mountain?

"Brock . . . ," I began, not knowing what to say.

It was too dark to see anything in the crawl space, but I could feel his eyes on me in the cramped space. Finally, after an eternity, he said, "I can help. I need to help."

I stared back, listening to the hopefulness in his breathing, my own breath caught in my throat. "Come on," I whispered as I turned toward the roof-access hatch.

After I slid around Aaren, I opened it a crack. When I didn't see anyone, I buttoned my coat, opened the hatch all the way, and crawled onto the flat roof. With the angled part of the roof behind me, I couldn't see anything on the other side of the building. But that meant they couldn't see me, either, so it was a good trade-off.

Twenty feet of snow-covered flat roof lay in front of

where I knelt, shaking from the cold, looking out into the early-morning darkness. The half-moon made everything glow a bluish-silver—bright enough to tell where we were going, but still dark enough to hide. From the height of the roof, I couldn't see anyone, but I could hear someone near the corner of the building, tapping his feet on the cobbled pathway like he was trying to stay warm.

Aaren and Brock crawled out of the hatch, while I inched toward the edge of the roof on my stomach. The Fours & Fives classroom was the easiest to climb down, so I hoped it wasn't within the line of sight of any bandits outside.

"See anything?" A gravelly voice startled me, and I crawled backward. It had come from the south end of the building—the end I couldn't see. The man belonging to the voice walked on the pathway below in our direction.

"Nope," a shivering bandit near us answered. "Who'd want to be out in this cold?"

"Not me," Gravel Voice said as he neared the middle of the building. "See you in ten."

Shivering Bandit dragged his feet as he walked, circling the building away from Gravel Voice.

"Now! We have to go now," I whispered. At any moment, the new bandit would reach the corner where he could see us. If we weren't quick enough, we'd have to wait another ten minutes. I crept to the edge of the roof, the wind blowing the powdery snow across my back. Then I lowered myself to the first foothold I could find in the bricks and climbed down. Brock and Aaren reached the bottom right after me, and we ran across the road and hid between my mom's bakery and the cannery as the bandit neared the corner of the Fours & Fives classroom.

The three of us peeked around the edge of the building. I didn't think the bandit saw us—he just looked cold. Like us. A stronger gust of wind blew the snow on the ground across the road, and he hugged his torso, then glanced around. He walked over to the tin shop and huddled under the roof overhang, shivering.

We did it! We were out, and things would be okay for everyone in the community center. I heaved a big sigh of relief.

We still had to travel east to get to the Hudsons' shed, which meant we needed to get past this bandit. I was about to suggest we stay close to the buildings where the snow wasn't deep, when a small thud pulled my attention to the ground at the side of the Fours & Fives classroom.

"Aaren?" A small voice carried on the wind. Brenna crouched next to the school, squinting into the darkness.

19

Escape

I glanced at Gravel Voice from around the corner of the cannery. I didn't think he could see Brenna from where he stood. But there was no way she could get to us, or that we could reach her without being seen. Aaren almost took off running toward her, but I grabbed his arm.

"If we get caught, it'll make things bad for everyone in there," I whispered.

Brock leaned close. "Wait until I distract the guard, then go get her." He took off behind the building, staying close to the edge. Not long after he disappeared behind the cannery, we heard a loud *thunk,* like a rock hitting wood, down past the tailor's shop.

"Did you hear that?" A voice came from the other end of the community center.

"Yeah," Gravel Voice called back. "I'll check it out." He pulled his hat down further, tugged his coat a little tighter around his neck, and trudged off toward the sound.

As soon as Gravel Voice disappeared from our sight, Aaren darted forward, the wind blowing the snow on the ground so much I could barely see him. He grabbed Brenna and carried her back to the cannery building. He put her on her feet, and the three of us ran along the wall at the back of the building toward Brock.

"Come on," Brock whispered as he motioned us toward the run-off ditch that wound around City Circle.

We climbed into the ditch, but the snow was so deep, it went to Brenna's waist. I lifted her up and shoved her into Brock's arms as soon as he got out of the other side of the ditch. When Aaren and I climbed out, we all raced toward the nearest building, the town stables. When I rounded the corner of the stable, I threw my back against the wall along with the others, panting.

"Were we seen?" I asked.

Brock peeked around the corner. "I don't think so."

"Are we gonna ride the horsies?" Brenna asked.

"No," Aaren whispered. "They'd make too much noise. Brenna, why didn't you stay with Mom and Dad?"

Brenna's voice sounded unsure and hurt. "Because . . . because you're my buddy. We're supposed to stay together."

"We have to get her to my family." Aaren's quiet voice

was on the verge of panic. "Maybe we can sneak back down."

"We can't," Brock said. "She'll have to stay with us."

I could feel waves of anger coming from Aaren. "She is *five*. This trip is too dangerous for her! We have to get her back."

"If we do, we'll get caught," Brock said. "If we get caught, there's no chance we'll get to Browning."

"She's my sister, Brock. How can you even suggest we take her?"

I knew Aaren's fear for Brenna was massive, because I'd never heard him talk in that voice to anyone. I couldn't think of anything to say to calm him.

Brock's voice came out surprisingly patient. "If we send her by herself, they might shoot her. If we find a way to return her, they'll still know she escaped when she suddenly shows up. They'll make her tell that we escaped, and that'd make things bad for her and your whole family. Hope's parents, too."

Brenna's entire body shook. She was probably scared and cold, so I hugged her close to me. I knew Brock was right. Taking her with us couldn't be worse than taking her back. I could tell that Aaren was considering it, too, because he'd stopped breathing like a caged wolf.

After a moment, Aaren whispered, "But I didn't even tell my parents that *I* was leaving."

Brock patted Aaren on the shoulder like he was proud of him, but I was speechless, and a little hurt. We were going to tell our parents.

Aaren looked at me like he was desperate for me to understand. "You saw how your dad reacted, Hope! My parents weren't going to be any different. I just figured when they saw that you and I were both missing, they'd talk to your parents to find out why. But now with Brenna—"

Maybe I did understand. I might have done the same thing. "So should we hide her somewhere?" I asked. "You could stay with her until the bandits are gone."

"If we don't walk constantly, we'll never stay warm without a fire, and the bandits will see the smoke." Aaren sighed. "Maybe we should take her."

"We'll keep her safe," Brock said.

"We will." I hoped I wasn't wrong.

We listened around the corner of the barn for any noises, but heard nothing. Being so close to them still made us nervous, so we ran. We didn't bother to hide our footprints—we just kept to places where people had already left tracks, and stayed off the roads. We cut through farms and yards for a little over a mile until we reached the Hudsons' house at the beginning of the third ring. We didn't see a single bandit along the way.

When we reached the shed, it was light enough to find the snowshoes, but it didn't occur to us until that moment that Mr. Hudson only had two sons. Which meant a total of three pairs of snowshoes. For four people. We'd have to carry Brenna.

We strapped the snowshoes to our backs with the laces meant to tie them to our feet and raced the next half mile to Aaren's and my houses. By the time we got there, we had frozen feet and numb fingers. Brock went with Aaren and Brenna to their house while I ran into mine. In my room, I peeled off my wet pants and socks, then yanked on two pairs of dry pants and three pairs of socks. I shoved my feet into my fur-lined boots, made sure my snowshoes were tied tightly on my back, and slung my schoolbag over my shoulder. Then I grabbed my full water skin off the kitchen counter and my gloves from the basket at the door, and went out the front door to get the others.

I stayed close to the low garden fence and snuck next door to Aaren's house. As I reached the corner of his house, I heard hoofbeats and a voice.

"Hey! There's a kid!" I turned to see three bandits riding our town's horses on the road that ran in front of my house, galloping toward me.

Distraction 20

"Aaren! Brock!" I screamed. "Bandits!"

Brock flung the front door open as I ran toward it. In the doorway, Aaren tugged Brenna's second glove on her hand and grabbed his slingshot, shoving it into his waistband, then we all ran.

"Up the hill!" I yelled. "They'll have a hard time following on the horses. We have to get to the orchard!"

We pounded across the packed snow of the road as the horses neared my house. As soon as we reached the snow-covered rise leading up to the fourth ring, Brock lifted Brenna and placed her on the hill as high as he could and shouted, "Go! Go!"

We didn't even try to walk up the steep incline—we

climbed, our hands and feet slipping in the deep snow as we struggled upward. We half pulled, half pushed Brenna as we went.

"Get them!" a bandit shouted just before he grabbed my ankle. Brock clambered past me and jerked Brenna out of the bandit's reach while I scraped my boot against my other ankle to shove the bandit's hand off. The yelling of the men, the neighing of the horses as their hooves beat against the hill, and Brenna's screaming all fueled my climb. I dug my fingers into the snow, grasping for any handhold that would help me get farther from them. One of the horses behind me rose up on its hind legs. I screamed and yanked Aaren to me just as the hoof came down, almost landing on his leg.

We scrambled the rest of the way up the hill as the men gave up trying to climb the hill and rode their horses away from us, toward the road a half mile back that led up to the fourth ring. When we reached the top of the hill, the men were already on the fourth ring, racing toward us.

I knew Brenna wouldn't be able to move fast enough, so I picked her up. The sound of my heart thundered in my ears, and I thought my lungs would burst before we made it to the orchard, but somehow we kept running, even after we reached the first trees. About ten rows in, I fell to my knees and Brenna tumbled to the ground. My lungs and my legs wouldn't let me take another step.

The horses stopped when they reached the edge of the orchard and reared anytime they neared the low, close branches.

"Should we go in?" One bandit's voice carried through the crisp air.

"No. This place's too big. We'll wait for them to come out." Then the bandit yelled, "You have to come out sometime!"

True, but at least I could catch my breath first.

I hadn't noticed how light it had become until the sun poked over the mountains and glittered on the snow through the trees. Brock pulled me to my feet and we walked through the orchard, thankful the trees had kept so much snow off the ground. Without discussing it, we all headed toward the big shed full of baskets and ladders at the end of the orchard that marked our usual path into the mountains.

Sometimes, when we headed home after sky jumping, the orchard felt five miles wide, even though it was less than one. Today, though, with the bandits constantly on the border of it, shadowing us, the end of the trees came fast. When Brenna said she was too tired to go any farther, we stopped to rest and get drinks of water. The bandits stopped, too, at the spot where we normally exited the orchard, the horses scraping their hooves impatiently on the ground. We were close enough that we could see their breath in the cold air.

Aaren put his water skin back into his bag. "How are we going to get out of here?"

"We only need to make it to the Bomb's Breath," I whispered. "They won't follow us through it."

Aaren nodded. "We need a distraction."

"I'll distract them," Brock said as he looked toward the men. "You go. Don't stop until you're past the Bomb's Breath."

Brock wasn't going to be the distraction. It was bad enough I brought more people than just myself on this trip, and I wasn't about to put any of them in extra danger.

"If I was the bad guys," Brenna said between drinks of water, "and I saw we didn't die in the Bomb's Breath, I'd still chase us. 'Cause I'm brave."

"Yes, you are." I looked at Aaren and Brock and raised an eyebrow. Brenna had a point.

"So we die," Aaren said simply.

I almost choked on the swig of water I was swallowing.

Aaren crouched down. "Brenna, when we get past the Bomb's Breath, do you think we can pretend to be dead and fool the bad guys?"

"I'm good at playing dead!" Brenna fell to the ground,

her eyelids fluttering and her tongue hanging out. Then she jumped to her feet again. "See?"

"Yes, you are good," Aaren said. "Um . . . when we fall to the ground, let's turn our faces *away* from the bad guys, okay?"

Brenna nodded like playing dead was the most exciting thing to happen to her all day.

"You ready?" Brock asked as he put his schoolbag strap over his head. His eyes were focused on the edge of the orchard, where he planned to create the distraction.

"Almost," I said. "Brock, will you help Brenna with her schoolbag?"

As he bent to pick up the bag, I stepped toward Aaren and whispered, "Get them to the Bomb's Breath." Before he could react, I grabbed the slingshot from his waistband and ran.

21
Slingshot

I hoped Brock wouldn't try to stop me from being the distraction. I was sure Aaren wouldn't—he knew me well enough not to try. I veered to the right to draw the men farther from where Brock, Aaren, and Brenna needed to exit the orchard. As I ran, I kept my eyes on the base of the trees, where there was almost no snow. Every few trees, I spied a leftover apple from autumn and picked it up. By the time I reached the edge of the orchard, I had four.

The bandits could tell I was trying to distract them, and they weren't buying it. Only one of the men rode down the edge of the orchard to deal with me.

He stopped twenty feet from me and lazily sized me up as I stepped out from the trees. I loaded a half-rotted, frozen apple into the sling. The bandit smiled like he knew the apple wouldn't hurt him.

But it wasn't meant to hurt. And it wasn't for him—it was for the horse he rode, Chance.

I pulled the apple back in the sling. The handle didn't feel right, and the band didn't stretch the same as mine at home, but at least I had a big target. I let go, and the apple sailed across the space between us. It wasn't a shot to win contests, but it hit Chance on his left shoulder. He reared, bucking the bandit right off his back before galloping away.

Normally, I hated that Chance would run off and leave his rider in a heap on the ground, and I refused to ride him if any other horse was available. Today, though, I wanted to kiss him.

The bandit stumbled to his feet, saying a bunch of words that would have made my mom cover my ears. By his limping steps in Chance's direction, I could tell that something hurt. Probably his tailbone. The man pulled out his gun, aimed at Chance, fired a shot, and missed. Chance ran without breaking stride, and the bandit yelled, "Miserable horse! You aren't worth the bullet I spent on you!"

I didn't hang around to see if he had another bullet to spend on me. I kept as close to the trees as I could, so he'd believe he had no chance of hitting me. As I ran along the edge of the trees toward the other bandits, I picked up five more apples. The others saw what had happened to their friend, so they held their reins tight and braced themselves. The one farthest from me was in charge, and gave the closer man orders to keep me in sight while he maneuvered nearer to Aaren, Brock, and Brenna. The three of them had stopped three rows in, unsure of what to do.

The closer man rode my favorite horse, Arabelle. I knew my apple wouldn't hurt, but I still felt bad. I took aim and hit her flank. She sidestepped. When I hit her with a second apple, though, she reared. The bandit slid off, landed on his feet, and grabbed Arabelle's reins to calm her. I hit her two more times quickly, and she ran. Her rider chose not to run after her.

Instead, he ran after me.

I cut back into the orchard. When I neared Aaren, Brock, and Brenna, I yelled, "Get to the Bomb's Breath!" I was so glad they had put their snowshoes on. At least they'd be able to escape quicker. As Brock and Aaren ran toward the fences, with Brenna on Brock's back, I ran alongside the edge of the orchard, slowing enough to take aim and shoot at the third rider's horse, even though it wouldn't make a difference. He rode Jack, the most even-tempered horse in White Rock, the one little kids learned to ride on.

When the apple hit, Jack flicked his tail but stayed calm. The second apple hit him in the leg, and he snorted but his rider soothed him by patting his neck and speaking softly. I figured Jack wouldn't run off, but at least I'd distracted his rider long enough for Aaren, Brenna and Brock to get to the fence. The man looked back to them just as they climbed over the warning fences, then he looked at me. By the expression on his face, he knew he couldn't go after all of us, but if he caught me, the others would come back for me.

He was probably right, which meant I couldn't get caught.

I slowed long enough to aim my next apple at the rider himself. He didn't stay as calm or as quiet as Jack did, but he didn't leave his horse to come into the orchard, either. The footfalls of the bandit chasing me sounded too close, so I didn't shoot my last apple. His legs were longer than mine. I needed an advantage over him and the guy on the horse.

The shed.

I ran like my life depended on it, which didn't take a lot of imagination. When I reached the edge of the orchard, the running bandit was so close I could hear his breathing, and the man on the horse closed in on me. The fifteen feet of open space between the orchard and the shed felt like a hundred as I ran. I flung the shed door open and made it inside moments before the rider and the running man caught up.

Apple boxes and baskets lay stacked and randomly strewn next to ladders, tree trimmers, and shovels. I knocked the stacks over as I ran to the opposite end of the shed, where shelves completely covered the wall except for the shuttered window you could prop open for sunlight.

The bandit behind me swore as he flung baskets and boxes against the wall, while the bandit on the horse yelled from the doorway, "Get her!"

The shed was dark enough that I doubted they knew the window was there until I climbed the shelves and threw open the shutters. I had planned to gracefully jump out of it, but when the bandit grabbed at my leg, I tumbled out and landed facedown in the snow.

I struggled to my feet and ran toward the warning fences. As I climbed the horizontal logs, I glanced over my shoulder. Both bandits chased me—one on foot and the other on horseback, and it was obvious he intended to jump the fence. I almost felt bad for the guy. Sure, his horse was the one most immune to slingshot apples, but Jack was meek in every way, including doing anything daring. Like jumping fences.

I had just made it past the bush we normally hid our

schoolbags under when I heard one bandit curse Jack's incompetence. Then fence boards creaked under the men's weight. Twice.

My lungs ached from breathing in the cold air while running. The snow was deep, and every step took so much energy, I wished I'd had time to untie my snowshoes from my back and put them on. Aaren, Brock, and Brenna plodded through the snow a hundred yards ahead of me, almost to the Bomb's Breath. I scrambled up the steep part and managed to yell between panting breaths, "They're coming!" I risked one look back at the men, even though I could hear their heavy breathing. The closer one wasn't more than a dozen feet behind me, and the two who had ridden Jack and Chance were not much farther behind.

When Aaren, Brenna, and Brock neared the Bomb's Breath, they sucked in a huge breath; then Aaren and Brock picked up Brenna and tromped up the mountain.

The Bomb's Breath was fifteen feet thick if you measured it straight up—like against the wall of the cliff we jump off. But when you climb a mountain, you don't go straight up, you go on an angle. So it was more like twenty-five or thirty feet. That isn't too far normally, but when you're trudging through a couple of feet of snow and can't take a breath, it sure is. When Aaren, Brenna, and Brock reached the boulder that meant they were beyond the Bomb's Breath, they fell to the ground.

I didn't think the bandits would have any trouble believing they were dead. They even looked dead to me. I let myself believe it long enough to yell a pained "No!" Then I filled my lungs with air and trudged through the Bomb's Breath. I'd never had such a hard time not breathing. With each clomping step in the deep snow, through pressurized air that took more energy to walk in than normal air, after running so long to get away from the bandits, I needed to breathe even more than usual.

When I finally reached the boulder above the Bomb's Breath, I felt like I was going to die.

22

Up the Mountain

I thought our plan to fake our deaths was brilliant, until I realized how difficult it would be after escaping. It was almost impossible to breathe shallowly when all I wanted to do was take great big heaving breaths.

I lay on my stomach in the snow and tried to pull enough air into my lungs without making my back rise, and without my breath showing up in the cold morning air. And without feeling like I was going to pass out.

The three men discussed whether we were actually dead, and if they should try to somehow drag us to their side of the Bomb's Breath to see. None of them were willing to get anywhere near it, though.

About the time my cheek, my arms, and the fronts of my legs became numb from the cold, the men decided that we must be dead, and that they should go back to the community center and tell Mickelson what happened. I heard the hooves of the horse and the crunching of at least one pair of boots in the snow, but I wasn't sure if I heard the second.

"Wake up, wake up," Brenna said in a singsong voice. "The bad guys are gone."

I opened my eyes and said a quick "Shh!" before I dared move.

"It's okay," she said. "We did it! We did it! We escaped!"

The bandits weren't in sight, though the cliff we normally jumped off blocked my view of everything downhill. I let out a huge breath of relief. They were gone!

"Come here, Brenna," Brock said. Brenna clambered onto his back, and he took a few steps. I couldn't believe how well the snowshoes worked.

I strapped on my snowshoes as quickly as possible. We walked up the mountain to where we usually sky jumped off the higher cliff, then we kept walking to the part of the mountain no one had stepped foot on before. It felt strange. It could have been the adrenaline from escaping the bandits, but it felt kind of exciting, too. We were doing something no one else had done.

I'd never used snowshoes before. They were wider and much longer than my shoes, but they actually kept me up on top of the snow. I had to walk like I'd spent too much time riding Arabelle, though, to keep each snowshoe from hitting my leg when I took a step.

We walked half a mile until we reached an area where lots of trees grew close together. The firs were much taller than they looked from the valley—the lowest branches were high enough that we could walk under most of them, and they kept almost all the snow off the ground.

"Do you wanna get down?" Brock asked Brenna.

"Yep," she said as she slipped to the ground. "I'll keep up. Because I'm really fast."

"You're probably faster than me," Brock said as we tied our snowshoes to our backs and walked under the tree canopy. Brenna ran ahead of us to prove him right.

"You're really good with her," Aaren said. "Thanks."

Brock just looked ahead. "She reminds me of my sister. They're the same age."

I was shocked to hear that he had a sister. The only other person I knew with the last name of Sances was Brock's grandpa. "Does she go to school?" I already knew the answer, but I asked anyway, hoping Brock would tell us more.

He looked sad and shook his head no.

Brock didn't start school until he was twelve, so maybe his sister didn't go to school for the same reasons. Carina was probably right about his dad. "Brock," I said, hoping my question wouldn't make him mad, "why don't you talk about your family? If your dad is a little crazy, that's okay."

Brock just looked at me for a few moments, like he was trying to decide whether to tell me. Then he shook his head and looked forward. "He's not. But that doesn't mean I want to talk about him." He pushed his hands into his coat pockets, his shoulders sagging again, and walked faster to catch up with Brenna. It made me wish I hadn't asked.

After a mile, the trees thinned and became shorter. Instead of almost all the ground being free of snow like it was through the trees, it was three feet deep everywhere. Because Brenna didn't have her own snowshoes, she'd no longer be able to walk. We figured it was a good place to stop for breakfast.

I opened the bag my mom had given me and laughed— she'd packed three of everything. I wondered if she had guessed the third person would be Brenna or Brock. The bag was filled with rolls, biscuits, dried meat, carrots, apples, raisins, and, wrapped in a dishcloth, three of my favorites—cherry pastries. We started with the pastries. That way they wouldn't get too squished on our journey. Each of us broke off a part of ours for Brenna. We all had our water skins, but since we still had so far to walk, we ate

drinking the water. Once our stomachs
r snowshoes were on our feet, we stared
n front of us.

u think it is to the Shovel?" Brock asked.

we stood, we had a clear view, and it looked
a lot bigger than our usual view of it from the valley.

Aaren shrugged. "Four hours? Five, maybe?"

I scoffed. "I bet we make it in two. Look how close it is!
It won't take us that long."

"It's not as close as you'd think," Aaren said. "Brenna,
come hop on my back."

"We can carry her," I said.

"I can do it." He winced as she climbed up, but he tried
to hide the pain. After adjusting Brenna on his back, he
started walking. Every step looked painful.

"I'll take her," I said, but he held on to her just a little
tighter. "Aaren—your stomach hasn't healed enough. I
can take her."

"We all have the same goal here, right?" Brock said.
"It doesn't matter who carries her, as long as we get there
safely."

Aaren heaved a defeated sigh, then let her slide off his
back. "Thanks."

We almost never stopped to rest as we headed toward
the top of the mountain. All it took for any of us to get over

feeling tired was a thought of my dad, or Mr. Hudson, or all the people who could get Shadel's soon.

I made sure to keep the Shovel in sight whenever trees or cliffs didn't block my way, but as we walked, the day grew darker instead of lighter. Dense storm clouds crowded the sky and blocked out the sun, making it even colder. The mountain rose steeper and steeper, with boulders or cliffs filling almost every space. Most were so big, we had to go around them. I wondered how crazy our footprints in the snow would look from above.

I didn't want Aaren to think it was hard to carry Brenna, so I kept her on my back for far too long. After an hour, every step was difficult, and my arm muscles were numb from holding her legs. I stopped to catch my breath, and Brock said, "Let me take her."

Brenna scooted around to my side, and I grabbed under her arms to pass her to Brock. I misjudged how exhausted my muscles were, and as Brenna's legs let go of my waist, I dropped her. We all screamed as she fell into the snow up to her ears; then she beat the snow away from her face.

"Are you hurt?" Aaren asked. "Can you stand up?"

"I *am* standing up!" Brenna jumped a little to show us.

I had never seen snow so deep before. We couldn't kneel to pull Brenna out or we'd sink, too. It took all three of us to pull her up. Once we finally got her onto Brock's back, I followed behind, brushing snow off Brenna and apologizing a million times.

It took forever to reach the Shovel—probably the four or five hours that Aaren had guessed it would take. Once we neared it, we discovered that the Shovel wasn't all the way at the top—it only looked that way from the valley. As snowflakes began to fall, Aaren pointed. "We should stop there for lunch before the weather gets worse."

Brock nearly collapsed as he set Brenna down. I'd been so exhausted when I handed her over to him, I had left him carrying her much longer than I should have. As soon as I opened the food bag, I handed Brock his portion first. He probably needed it the most after that. We ate biscuits, dried meat, and apples, while keeping an eye on the thick clouds overhead. They made me nervous. At least the cliff face of the Shovel kept most of the wind and snow off us.

Aaren looked around the edge of the Shovel toward the top of the mountain, then at the sky. "We need to go. *Now.*"

We packed what was left of our lunch and slung our bags over our shoulders. We'd all been caught in enough snowstorms to know we needed to move. I adjusted Brenna's hood to make sure it covered her ears and pulled her coat sleeves over her gloves, then did the same for mine. Our coats were warm—hopefully warm enough. I just wished they covered our legs, too.

I crouched down so Brenna could climb on my back.

"Ready?" Aaren asked.

I hiked Brenna a little higher and got a good hold of her legs. "Yep." We all took a deep breath and stepped into the wind as it blew the snow toward us in sheets. The snow felt like hundreds of needles stabbing my skin. Brenna nuzzled her face into the back of my neck. The wind blew against me so hard, making each step seem like I was staying in the same place. I leaned into the snow and pushed myself even more.

It took less than thirty minutes after we left the Shovel to reach the top of the mountain, even though it felt farther than the entire distance we'd come. I was frozen and everything hurt, but a flutter of excitement still ran through me as I thought about looking over the crest and seeing Browning, especially from so high up. To see what was outside the valley I'd spent almost my entire life in.

The wind drowned out all sounds except the beating of my heart in my ears. I stepped onto the crest to look past the miles of mountain below me, to where I knew the plains must begin. To where I knew Browning's houses were close together, inside tall dirt walls in the shape of a square. As I looked out, I saw no color, no forms, and certainly not distance. The only thing in sight was the obscuring white of the worst blizzard I had ever seen.

Brenna in Danger

The landscape was much rougher than on our side of the mountain, which made the blinding blizzard a huge problem. There were so many times we almost walked into the sheer face of a cliff, a section of forest that was impassable, or a drop-off too steep to climb down, then had to backtrack to find a different path. I felt guilty every time I led us in a direction that made us turn around. We had far enough to go without zigzagging our way down the mountain.

And then there was the issue of the Bomb's Breath. I had made a mental note of how long it had taken us to travel from the Bomb's Breath on White Rock's side of the mountain to the top. I had planned to go that same distance down the outside of the mountain before starting to feel around for the Bomb's Breath. With all our backtracking, though, I had no idea how far we were from it. I kept trying to look behind us toward the top of the mountain, to figure out how far we'd come, but I couldn't see more than a yard's distance through the blizzard. And my feet felt so heavy, especially in the snowshoes, that I wasn't sure I'd even notice if I stepped right into the Bomb's Breath. And if we couldn't tell when we walked into it, we could die.

I'd never been so cold in all my life. It had been forever since I last had feeling in my fingers or toes, or even my arms and legs. I constantly worried I'd drop Brenna.

I stumbled to a stop when Brock grabbed my shoulder. "I'll take her for a bit."

I nodded and numbly handed Brenna to him. The helplessness in Aaren's eyes as he looked at us was too much. "Don't," I said. "We've got her."

Brock studied me for a moment. "We should rest."

"I agree," Aaren said.

Nothing sounded better than curling up in the soft snow and sleeping until I was warm again. I pushed my schoolbag behind me now that Brenna wasn't on my back and started walking before the idea of a rest settled in my mind. "We can't," I said, my lips feeling almost too numb to talk. "Only thing keeping our muscles warm is using them. We stop, our muscles freeze and we die."

No one questioned me—they just followed.

*   *   *

We kept plodding ahead. My muscles were probably sore, so I was grateful my legs were numb. At least I had Brenna on my back again—it was nice to have her warmth and her chatter.

I wished I had a free hand to rub the stone on my necklace. My birth parents came to White Rock during a snowstorm like this when my mom was pregnant with me. Their town had been attacked by bandits, and almost no one escaped. My birth dad knew the storm and the trip could kill them, but he wanted to get me to safety. The snow was deep, but the wind hadn't blown many drifts yet, so they were able to make it through the tunnel. Their trip had been so hard that as soon as my dad got my mom to White Rock, he died. My mom went into labor soon after that and died moments after giving birth to me. Everyone was shocked that my birth parents had made it to White Rock during such a terrible storm. But they did. And their trip was a lot longer than our trip to Browning. If they could do it, I could, too.

I concentrated on moving my feet. But in the back of my mind, I knew I'd forgotten something. Something I needed to pay attention to. Every time I tried to figure it out, I found myself looking down. It was mesmerizing to watch my feet move ahead, one right after another. *Step, step.*

Step, step.

Step, step.

A gust of wind blew past us, causing my breath to catch in my throat. For a brief moment, the snow cleared and I saw farther than usual. In front of us rose cliffs, large boulders, and thick trees. A few hundred yards to the left, though, a treeless, boulderless path ran alongside a cliff face, like a safe passageway. Finally, we caught a break! I breathed a sigh of relief and led the way to the path down the mountain.

Each time the snow cleared a bit, the way downhill looked as smooth as the snowy path we walked on. Cliffs rose on both sides of us, and the ground up there was uneven and covered in trees. I was grateful we traveled on this path instead of backtracking through either of those areas.

Brenna shivered a lot, like the last time she was on my back, but she wasn't as chatty. I squeezed her legs. "You okay?"

"Isss sooo cooode," she whispered.

I knew that walking kept our muscles warm, but it hadn't occurred to me until right then that Brenna wasn't keeping her muscles warm. I wished we had snowshoes for her so she could walk. Her feet crossed at my stomach, so I pulled my coat up over them as much as possible, and covered her legs with my arms as much as I could.

"She's slurring her speech," Aaren murmured.

"Hypothermia. The brain's sensitive to cold." He gave her a drink of water, then adjusted her hood to cover her head better.

I rubbed her legs, hoping the friction would help warm her. "We need to find trees close together, like the ones on our side of the mountain. Somewhere without much snow. There has to be a place where she can get down and walk a little."

Brock looked around. Our perfect pathway didn't have many trees.

"Soon, Brenna." Aaren kissed her forehead. "Soon. You'll be okay."

Except it didn't seem soon. And she didn't seem okay. It took an hour before we found a place where the cliff jutted out and had an overhang, blocking snow from falling and winds from blowing any snow. Before we reached it, Brenna stopped shivering. I knew she was in trouble. "Brenna?"

No answer.

Under the overhang, Aaren gasped in pain as he lifted her off my back. He tried to get her to stand up, but she was so sick. Her face was pale and her lips were blue. I looked to Aaren for reassurance, but I think he was even more scared than I was. He moved her limp arms around to try to get her muscles warm.

He looked ahead, as if he could actually see through

the storm, then bit his lip. "This isn't enough—she's getting bad. We have to find a way to keep her warmer!"

"Think you'll fit into my coat?" I asked.

Aaren didn't answer; he just took his off. I set my bag on the ground, then unbuttoned my coat and switched with him. His was a hand-me-down from Travin and was a little too big for him, which meant it was a lot too big for me. I shook some life back into my hands.

"Do you want me to carry her?" Brock asked.

My arms were so tired, but I had to have Brenna near me, to know she was okay. I shook my head no. "She's like my sister. I have to carry her."

I expected Brock to argue, but instead he nodded like he understood completely. He took out the contents of his bag—a water skin, his bale-grabber invention, and the remnants of his lunch—and put them into mine; then he pulled out his knife and cut at his bag. I bent down and picked up Brenna, hugging her to the front of me with her legs wrapped around my back.

"Wait," Brock said. He stabbed his knife into the bag's strap at one end, then pulled it all the way to the other end, turning it into two straps. He'd already cut the base of the bag enough that it could no longer be used as a bag.

I stared at it, dumbfounded, even after Aaren said, "Good idea. That'll work great."

Brock put one strap over each of my shoulders. The

bottom of the bag—the part I thought was ruined—he slipped under Brenna's behind. Like a sling, it transferred her weight from my arms to my shoulders. Now my exhausted arms wouldn't have to work so hard, and I didn't have to worry about dropping her. And I could scratch my nose if I needed to.

"Wow, thanks," I said. Having people around who could invent sure was handy. Aaren helped me put on his coat, and made sure the back of it covered Brenna's legs. Brock buttoned it so that except for the top of her head, Brenna was completely inside the coat I wore. I felt her breath against my neck, barely there, and I looked at Aaren in alarm.

Tears were forming in his eyes, and his forehead creased with worry.

"How bad will she get if she's not warm enough?" I asked. Aaren didn't answer—he just swallowed hard. By the look on his face, I wasn't sure I could handle hearing the answer anyway.

We walked as fast as we could. We hadn't been able to see the sun for—I had no idea how long, but it must have set, because the sky grew even darker. I hugged Brenna to me tighter.

We couldn't see far ahead, so I was shocked when our pathway ended at a thirty-foot drop-off. I stood on the edge of the cliff and looked down to where the path continued at the base of the cliff, with no trail leading to it.

Brock looked behind us at the rock walls on both sides of the path we'd traveled. "It'll take hours to walk back that entire distance, uphill, to find another way down. If there even is another way."

Aaren shook his head. "We don't have hours!"

I just stared at the drop-off and thought about how I never, not in a million years, imagined I'd be grateful for this storm. Until now.

24
First Jump

That was the thing that had been tickling the edges of my mind. The Bomb's Breath.

As I looked off the edge of the cliff, I could actually *see* it. The falling snowflakes slowed the moment they touched it. Almost like time had frozen just over the edge.

My first thought was to jump off the cliff and continue walking down our path. It was just that Aaren hadn't sky jumped since he'd cut his stomach. And I had never jumped with someone in my arms before. And Brenna had never jumped at all, and even if she was awake, she might be too sick to follow directions. But I didn't see another choice. I raised an eyebrow and looked to Aaren and Brock. "You guys up for a jump?"

Brock shrugged. "We won't be able to land standing up. The ground's not flat."

"We could land on our backs and slide," I said. "Think we can do it?"

Aaren squinted over the edge. "I can't see far enough to tell if the path is clear. That could be a problem." He turned to look up the mountain. "But if it's like the way we came, it might be fine. We could dig our snowshoes into the snow to stop ourselves from hitting a tree or going off another cliff. I think." He looked at Brenna and bit his lip.

"You hate that she has to do something dangerous when she's so sick," I whispered.

He changed the subject. "Will you be able to see over Brenna to tell where you're going when you're on your back?"

I shook my head.

Brock stepped next to me. "Then we'll go down together."

"Okay," I said. "Together."

Brenna slept on my shoulder, so I gave her a squeeze to wake her up. I knew if I covered her mouth and nose while she was asleep, instinct would make her fight to breathe, and that would be deadly in the Bomb's Breath. I told her what we were about to do, unbuttoned my coat and shifted her in the sling so that her back was against my left arm and her legs were curled up on my stomach instead of around my waist, then buttoned my coat again. "Are you excited you didn't have to wait until you were ten for your first jump?"

Her eyes were barely open, but she nodded. I hoped she was alert enough.

Aaren linked arms on my left and Brock on my right. We stepped up to the edge of the cliff and took a deep breath. I covered Brenna's mouth and nose; then we jumped into the sky. We fell at least ten feet before we hit the Bomb's Breath, and Brenna's eyes were wide open in fear the whole time.

And then we hit the Bomb's Breath and everything slowed. Every bit of worry and exhaustion left my body. I just floated on an invisible cloud. My worries felt as weightless as my body. Snowflakes lazily drifted all around me as excitement flurried in my stomach. Brenna was snuggled into me, Aaren's and Brock's shoulders rested against mine, and for that moment, everything was right. My smile must have looked downright blissful to Brenna, because she relaxed as she looked into my eyes. I could think of nothing I'd rather do than spend the day sky jumping.

Except, of course, saving my town and saving Brenna. We kicked our legs to move to a lying-down position. I soaked in the feeling of weightlessness for another moment before we touched down on the sloped ground at the base of the cliff as gently as the snowflakes did.

We slid slowly at first, but when we went downhill enough to exit the Bomb's Breath, we slid really fast. I took a deep breath and just trusted Aaren and Brock to guide us, and told Brenna how good she did on her first jump. She gave me a weak smile that I think meant she loved it.

The hood of Aaren's coat didn't fit me well, so after only a moment, it blew off my head. The snow and wind from going so fast blew through my hair and bit into my scalp, freezing my skull. I wondered if the massive pain in my head was from my brain itself shivering.

I tried not to flinch every time Aaren and Brock yelled to one another right before one of them kicked to change our direction. Instead, I ignored the snow blowing into my face and told Brenna that this was the world's best sledding run because we didn't have to climb back up—we just got to keep going down. But the thought that we wouldn't be able to stay in Browning long before we'd have to go back into this cold wasn't far from my mind. "Just enjoy the ride," I said, as much to myself as to Brenna.

Brenna didn't enjoy the ride. Her eyes closed and her breathing was either shaky or shallow. I didn't know much about hypothermia, but the color of her face wasn't normal. I was grateful we were moving so fast.

About the time the pain from the snow inside my coat and the wind on my bare head became worse than I could handle, we reached the bottom of the mountain and slid to a stop halfway up a hill.

Brock and Aaren brushed the snow out of the inside of my coat, scooped as much snow out of my hood as they could, then put my hood back on. It didn't feel any warmer. I looked at Aaren. My coat wasn't big enough for him, so the hood didn't cover him well, either. I bet his head was just as cold as mine. Brenna seemed comfortable enough curled into a ball at my stomach, so I didn't move her. I didn't have the energy to do it anyway.

We climbed to the top of the hill just to see another one waiting.

"There's more?" Aaren asked, his voice desperate.

"A lot more," Brock said. "The bomb left hills circling the crater that White Rock is in. Kind of like the ripples you get when you drop a rock in the lake. The hills get smaller as we get farther away from the mountain, though."

"You've been here?" I asked through frozen lips that could barely move.

He nodded.

"I have, too," I said. "Well, not *here,* of course. But on the road from White Rock to Browning. I think I was asleep the whole time, though—I don't remember it at all."

"Think we're close?" Aaren asked, slurring his words.

Brock squinted into the distance. "I'm guessing we're not."

I lost control of my legs. Or maybe I'd walked so much my legs forgot how to do anything else. Just like I forgot what being warm felt like. And the sky forgot how to do anything other than dump snow.

No traces of daylight remained, but because of the moonlight and the fact that everything around us was white, we could see.

I was exhausted and my head hurt so much from the cold, I didn't think I could go any farther. Every time I wanted to quit, I'd focus on something in the distance. A tree. The top of a hill. A big lump of snow. And then I'd say to myself, *I can make it that far.* And when I got there, Brock or Aaren would put a hand on my back, or we'd go downhill—something that felt like a little push, and I'd keep going. And going. And going.

When the urge to stop got really bad, I chanted with each step. *Save Brenna,* step. *Save my dad,* step. *Save White Rock,* step.

Aaren grabbed hold of my shoulder, so I stopped for him to check on Brenna. "Sheanybetter?" I asked, my words not coming out right.

"No. Maybe when she fell, snow got under her coat and melted against her body and made her clothes wet. That'd keep her from getting warm. Or maybe you aren't warm enough to warm her. Or maybe isss just too cold out here."

"Are we even going the right direction?" I asked. "What if Browning's that way, or that way, and we just pass it by?" I wanted to give up. I didn't know what made me think I could hike over a mountain I had never traveled on before, and find a city covered in snow that I'd only been to one time nine years ago when I was too young to remember anything. And I'd brought Aaren and Brenna and Brock with me, endangering us all.

Aaren's shoulders slumped. "What are we going to do?"

"Look!" Brock pointed into the distance. "There it is!"

City Walls

25

"See those white lumps?" Brock asked. I squinted into the distance and could kind of see two hills through the falling snow, right next to each other. "Those are the greenhouses where Browning grows the cotton. So the farmlands must be just beyond this next hill."

"Maybe iss just hills." I thought of the two greenhouses we had in White Rock between the orchard and the cattle. These were huge, easily ten times the size of ours.

"It has to be them," Brock said.

"Thass good," Aaren said, "'cause you're slurring your words, Hope."

"So are you, Aaren," Brock said.

Aaren pulled the too-small hood of my coat tighter. "Brains can't handle cold. Muddles your thinking."

With my brain working so slowly, I didn't remember about Browning's dirt walls in the shape of a square until we were most of the way across the farmlands. Something looked like another hill, except that it wasn't long and spread out like the ripples from the crater or in lumps like the greenhouses. We might have totally missed it if Brock hadn't reminded us what we were looking for. I was glad at least one of our brains worked. My sense of time was off, too, but Brock said it was about ten p.m., which meant we'd been traveling for seventeen hours.

The fifteen-foot-high snow-covered wall around Browning was sloped on the outside. I looked down at Brenna, asleep in the sling. I wished she was awake to see it.

"Iss so short," Aaren slurred. "Don't you think it's short?"

I nodded yes. We had mountains as our city walls. This definitely felt short.

"I heard that before the bombs, no one had city walls," Aaren said.

"Yeah, well, they didn't have bandits back then," Brock said as he grabbed my shoulders and directed me alongside the dirt wall instead of over it like I was trying. "This way. You'll break a leg if you go over here—we have to get to the gate."

I followed Brock as he muttered something about

Aaren's and my brains being frozen solid. After ten minutes, we reached a locked gate but no guards manned it. Brock guessed they might be rotating guards or covering a larger than normal area because of the snow. Someone would probably be back soon, but we had to get Brenna by a warm fire quickly. My mind was so tired and cloudy, though, I couldn't figure out what we should do.

Just beside the gate, Brock had us climb up the dirt wall. At the top, a wooden guard platform sat slightly lower than the wall, with the edge two feet away and a fifteen-foot drop-off between it and the dirt wall. Only a couple of inches of snow covered the platform, so it must have been shoveled, and footprints showed someone had been there not long before. Brock jumped to the platform and slid on the snow a bit, then held out his hand for me. It was a big step between the wall and the platform, and with Brenna strapped to me, I didn't want to take any chances. I reached forward and grabbed his hand with my right, then reached back for Aaren's hand with my left. Brock pulled me across, then Aaren joined us and we climbed down the ladder.

The inside walls went straight up. They weren't dirt—in some places they were tall timbers placed right next to each other, or stone, or cement, or huge pieces of some kind of metal that must have existed before the bombs. Somewhere in my frozen brain, I wondered how far they'd traveled to scavenge them, and how hard it was to stand them on end.

And then I wondered how long I'd stared at this tall wall that enclosed an entire city, because Brock's voice was urgent. "Come *on*, Hope! We have to keep moving!" He grabbed me by one hand and Aaren by the other and led us down a street.

The houses stood close together in neat lines. The intersecting roads were straight, too, like the city was set up as a giant grid. Some houses were bigger than others, and they were different colors, but they all looked cozy. And I'd have bet they had nice soft beds in them. And warm food. If it weren't for Brock pulling me, I'd have opened one of their doors and collapsed in front of one of their fires. He was probably looking for the guard barracks. I bet they had fires and warm food and soft beds there, too.

"There's no one here," Aaren said as we walked.

Sometimes we saw footprints, and the snow had been partly shoveled in some areas, but we didn't see guards, and no one came out of their houses.

"They're here," Brock said. "The blizzard is just too thick. And the snow muffles sound. The people in their homes probably haven't heard us over the crackling of their fires."

I glanced at a bluish house. If I were in there, I wouldn't open my shutters for anything. I'd just curl up next to the fire. I kissed Brenna's cold forehead and whispered, "We'll be warm soon."

We walked past so many houses, I no longer cared if we made it to the guard barracks first. I just wanted to be by a fire. But Brock kept pulling us, so we kept following. Finally, we walked up to the door of a soft green house with a dark brown wooden door and dark brown shutters. Yellow light shone through the cracks. Firelight. My whole body tingled in anticipation of that fire. Brock let go of my hand and knocked on the door, and a girl about our age, with hair as dark as Brock's, answered. When she saw us, her eyes lit up.

"Mom, Estie, Stephen, Max! It's Brock! Brock is home!"

26 Family

With my fuzzy brain, I couldn't understand why the girl had said Brock was home. Brock lived in White Rock.

"Hey, Linet," Brock said as he gave her a hug. Her dark hair fell in a braid halfway down her back. Brock told us to come into the house, while two dark-haired boys wearing pajamas ran into the room. One was about eight years old and one about ten, and they both looked like they'd been asleep. All of them had the same gemlike green eyes as Brock. I just stared as they hugged him.

"They're his family?" I whispered to Aaren.

"Have to be," he whispered back. "They look just like him."

My attention was drawn to a clicking sound. A little girl with straight dark hair that barely touched her shoulders—probably the five-year-old sister Brock had talked about—hobbled into the room on little wooden crutches. The mom walked next to the girl until she saw Brock; then she ran to wrap her arms around him.

"Brock! My goodness, Brock." Her voice was gruff, but somehow kind at the same time. She put her hands on his cheeks and then his shoulders. "You all look like death, being out in a storm like this!" She turned to her children. "Stephen, put more logs on the fire. Max, make some hot cider, please. Linet, put some soup on."

"Brock, why—" When she looked back to us, her eyes fell on me and she gasped. She could hardly see Brenna, so she must have known there was a problem by our expressions.

"She has hypothermia," Brock said. "It's bad."

She unbuttoned my coat, then took Brenna from my arms. "Poor baby," she said. As she walked toward the fire, she felt Brenna's forehead and pulled up her eyelids.

Aaren hovered near Brenna with his forehead crinkled and his voice hoarse. "Can you help her?"

"We'll fix her up. Don't you worry." Brock's mom laid a blanket in front of the fire, then placed Brenna on it. She was so sick, she didn't even move at all. "Stephen, her clothes are wet. Get Estie's warmest clothes. Quickly."

Max came into the room with mugs of hot cider and gave us each one.

"Is there any hot water on the stove?" Brock's mom asked.

Max nodded.

"Put it in a water skin, then put more water on to heat."

When that mug of hot cider was pressed into my hands, my whole body celebrated the warmth. As I sipped it, the heat went all the way down my throat and into my stomach. I sipped some more, and wished that Brenna felt well enough to drink. I took off my coat and laid it in front of the fire so it would start to dry, then moved as close to the fire as I could without getting burned.

Within moments, Brock's mom had changed Brenna into dry clothes, put the water skin with warm water on her chest, and wrapped the blanket around her. She was humming a lullaby into her ear while she cradled her in front of the fire as if Brenna were her own child.

Brock's mom had the same straight dark hair as Brock and his siblings, pulled into a ponytail. The hair that had escaped the ponytail fell by her cheeks and made her green eyes even brighter. Tiny pieces of light blue string covered her shirt and pants, but they somehow belonged. Like the way my mom always had flour on her from making pastries.

As soon as he saw that his mom was taking care of Brenna, Brock's focus went to Estie. Her crutches knocked on the floor as she moved as fast as she could to where Brock sat.

Brock hugged her, and she sat on his lap. "I missed you, Estie!" he said.

"I missed you, too. Are you back? Back for good?"

She was so sweet and her voice sounded so hopeful—and Brock's face looked so sad as he shook his head no—it made me want to tell her, *Yes! Brock is back and will never leave again!* But instead, Brock changed the subject. "How long have you had these cool crutches?"

He glanced at his mom, and she gave him a sad smile. "About two months."

Brock turned back to his sister. "Wow. Only two months, and already you're an expert. You've always been my Speedy Estie."

I'd tried to imagine what Brock's family was like more times than I could count. Never did I picture any of this. I stared at Brock as he held Estie with a look on his face I hadn't seen before. But the change wasn't only in his face. His shoulders were square—like the weights that always pulled them down weren't there.

Aaren's focus went from Brenna to Estie every few seconds, like Estie was a puzzle he couldn't figure out. Then his eyes widened and he gasped. Brock looked at him, and Aaren said quietly, "My mom came to see Estie during the Planting Festival."

Brock nodded.

"I—I'm sorry," Aaren said. "I've heard my mom talk about her. I never knew it was your sister."

Brock ignored Aaren and started playing a clapping game with Estie.

Aaren turned to me and whispered, "She has a tumor on her spine that's growing. Eventually it will paralyze her if they can't remove it."

The clapping game continued, but after a moment, Brock looked at Aaren again. Aaren said in a voice so convincing I would have believed him if he said it was a hot, sunny day outside, "My mom will find a cure. I know she will."

Brock stared at Aaren, then gave him a quick nod and turned his focus back to Estie.

Behind me, a couch and a couple of chairs formed a U shape around the fire, and a pedal-operated sewing machine and stand that must have been made before the bombs stood against one wall. A long table ran along the opposite wall, covered with yards of blue cotton fabric, the same kind my school shirts were made of. Several stacks of the fabric, cut and ready to be sewn, lay near the sewing machine. Piles of the shirts, finished except for the hem, sat on the couch next to a spool of thread and a pincushion.

I knew Browning made almost all our clothing, and

that we traded food for it. It worked for everyone, because food grew really well in White Rock, and Browning had those giant greenhouses to grow cotton in. I'd just never thought about the people who sewed the clothes. I hadn't imagined a family sitting around the fire, each doing their part to help make what I wore. I definitely hadn't pictured Brock's family doing it. I looked at my own shirt and wondered if maybe it had once been cut pieces of fabric, sitting in a pile on the floor of Brock's house, waiting to be sewn.

Linet stepped back into the room and sat on the couch. She picked up a blue shirt and the needle and thread from the pincushion and began to hem the bottom of it, as if it wasn't natural to sit without sewing.

"Now, Brock," his mom said as she removed the water skin from Brenna's torso and gestured for Stephen to refill it with warmer water. "I know you didn't come all the way here during a blizzard just to say hello. What happened?"

"Mom," he said, "these are my friends Hope, Aaren, and Brenna."

"Friends?" A smile spread across Linet's face. "You owe me a week's worth of hemming." She turned to us. "I made him a bet before he left. *I* said that within a week, his first friend would be a girl, because he'd miss me so much he couldn't stand it," she teased. "*He* said it would never happen."

Since our faces were still red and frozen, it was hard to tell, but I think Brock blushed. "Aaren, Hope—I'd like you to meet my twin sister, Linet."

"Um, hi," I said. "I'm the first friend he made who's a girl."

Linet looked back and forth between us and grinned. Then her eyes got wide and she gasped. "You like her!" she said to Brock.

"What?" Brock and I practically yelled at the same time.

"You like her," Linet said again. "I can tell by that look on your face!"

Brock's face turned redder and redder, and by how hot mine felt, I imagined it looked pretty red, too. Brock's mom saved us, though.

"Linet. Now's not the time for teasing." She gave me a look that apologized for Linet. "We need to hear what happened."

Brock looked relieved at the change in subject. He explained to his mom what had happened with the bandits, how my dad said he was in charge and got shot, about the antibiotics, the deadline, our trip over the mountain, and that an outbreak of Shadel's Sickness might be on its way.

The more the fire warmed me, the clearer my mind

became. All I'd been able to focus on during our trip was getting to Browning. Now my thoughts overwhelmed me. I couldn't sit for another second. "We have to go. Right now—we have to go tell the guard." I grabbed my coat, which wasn't nearly dried out enough yet, and put it on.

Brock and Aaren stood up, too, but Aaren seemed less sure of himself.

"Go," Brock's mom said. "Do what you have to do. The soup and a warm fire will be waiting for you when you get back." She looked at Aaren. "Don't worry. We'll take good care of your sister."

As we stepped through the doorway and into the blizzard, a gust of wind hit, and my body shivered violently. The ten minutes we'd spent in Brock's house had taken the sting off the cold, but I still felt frozen to the middle of my bones. I hadn't slept much last night; then we'd walked, hiked, run, or slid over and down the mountain for seventeen hours. I wanted to sleep in a warm bed, not freeze on my way to convince Stott to load everyone up and go to White Rock with us.

This was Stott's first year as Captain of the Away Guard. The Away Guard was usually just single young men—once people had families, they weren't interested in leaving them for months at a time. Even so, guards never got promoted to captain so young. It had only been two years since Stott graduated from Sixteens & Seventeens. For as long as I'd known him, people had done anything he asked. Probably because he was fiercely protective of everyone.

At the end of Brock's road, we turned onto a street with houses almost exactly like the ones we'd just passed. I had a million questions to ask Brock about his family and his home, and even about whether Linet was right and he did like me, but I needed to think about what I'd say to the captain. I didn't know how I'd be able to talk him into taking all of his men through the Bomb's Breath, so instead I focused on figuring out the details of our trip. We'd left White Rock at five a.m., and we didn't reach Browning until ten p.m. My cold brain worked through the math slowly. Mickelson had said the town had until sunset tomorrow, so we'd have to leave by midnight or sooner to make it back in time.

Hopelessness washed over me. I couldn't do it. I couldn't turn around and make that same journey again in a little over an hour. Brock and Aaren looked as haggard as I felt. I wasn't sure any of us could make it.

Brock led us through snow-covered streets to a long gray stone building he said was the barracks. The door was unlocked, so we walked inside. Bunk beds lined the walls on both sides, covered with quilts in a variety of colors. Round tables sat in the wide aisle down the middle.

Twenty guards, including Aaren's brothers Cole and Travin, looked up from their spots around the tables, where they played Empty Basket with homemade dice. Their expressions quickly turned from indifference to recognition, then to alarm. Everyone got to their feet—several so fast, they knocked their chairs over. They weren't stupid. They knew we wouldn't have shown up in their building unless White Rock was in trouble.

27
Staying Behind

"What's going on?" Stott demanded as he walked into the main area from his office at the back. All sound in the building died as Stott's eyes met ours and his face paled. The look was confirmation enough for the men. The room became as chaotic as snowflakes blowing in every direction. A low buzz of whispers filled the space as the men scrambled to their packs and supply closets. Cole and Travin stood frozen, like they couldn't decide whether to rush to their own packs or to their brother.

Stott motioned us to his office, where he sat behind a wooden desk. "Have a seat."

His eyes bored into us as he scratched at the stubble on his chin. "I'm guessing your parents didn't exactly give you permission to come here."

I glanced at Aaren. "Not exactly."

He nodded once. "Bandits?"

"Yes."

"Bandits in the winter *in* White Rock." Stott shook his head and spoke with a tight voice. "While we sat here, our services barely needed beyond making sure people have enough firewood. How bad is it?"

We took turns telling all that had happened. Stott stayed quiet the whole time.

"So," I said, "to make it over the mountain and to the community center in time, we have to leave soon."

Stott leaned back in his chair. "I'm not taking my men over the mountain."

Heat rose all through my body, especially in my face. "How can you say that? They've threatened to kill people if we don't give them all our Ameiphus! And then they'll probably take the Ameiphus anyway! My dad will die. Mr. Hudson will die. Melina too."

"I didn't say we wouldn't help," Stott said. "Just that I won't take my men over the mountain. Every single one of them is brave, Hope. They're ready to walk out that door right now and put their lives on the line to save White Rock. But you know as well as I do that there isn't a man in there who'd go anywhere near the Bomb's Breath, whether they knew you three could go through it or not. How'd the bandits get in?"

"There's a hole in the mine floor that leads to the river," Aaren said.

Stott nodded. "Then we'll go around the outside of the crater to the west side and enter through the same cave." He looked at each of us. "But none of you look able to make the trip. I recommend you stay behind, recover, and travel back home when it's over."

We stood up and protested loudly.

He stared at us for a long while, probably thinking about our parents' reactions to finding out we were gone and, knowing Stott, how much he'd hate being left behind if he were us. Eventually he let out a huge exhale. "Okay. I'll get you back. But once we reach White Rock, you will stay far from City Circle until the problem is resolved."

"Stott?" Aaren said quietly. "Brenna came, too. She's back with Mrs. Sances, recovering from hypothermia."

Stott's jaw flexed as he ground his teeth. "We'll put her on a horse. That's the best I can do." He stood up. "I need to ready my men. We leave at four a.m."

I'd be able to sleep soon, in a warm bed, and we'd still get to White Rock in time. Four hours of sleep didn't seem like much, but since I hadn't expected I'd get any, it sounded like heaven.

As soon as the barracks doors shut behind us and I was no longer worried about how to convince the guard to join us, I blurted to Brock, "Why are you living in White Rock if your family's here?"

Brock kept his head down, and for a moment, I thought he wouldn't answer. Then he looked at me and laughed. "I can't believe you waited so long to ask! I thought you would as soon as we got to my house."

I laughed, too, and gave him a playful shove. "Just tell us."

"My dad grew up in White Rock. He was my grandpa's only child. After he finished Sixteens and Seventeens, my dad joined White Rock's guard. He was promoted to Captain of the Away Guard just before his third winter. He was the first one to make captain as young as Stott did," Brock said with pride. "During his first winter as captain, he met my mom. He stayed in Browning, they got married, and he joined Browning's guard."

I thought back to the hermit we'd guessed was Brock's dad. Now that I'd actually met Brock's family, it seemed so silly.

"My dad said he'd give his life for this town." Brock was silent for a few minutes and looked up at the falling snow as we walked. When he spoke again, it was a whisper. "And he did. He was shot by bandits when Estie was a baby. Lots attacked at once. My dad and two other guards died, but they saved Browning."

So we both had fathers willing to die for their town. We both had fathers who were shot by bandits. The difference was, mine was still alive. Yes, I'd snuck out to save all the people of White Rock, but a big part of me did it to save my dad. I hadn't asked Brock to come, but I still felt pangs of guilt that he was helping to save my dad when there was no way to save his.

Brock led us down another street. "Last spring, when people from White Rock were here for the Planting Festival, we found out that my grandpa's arthritis was so bad he couldn't do things himself. He needed help, so my mom decided it would be best to move to White Rock. We could take care of my grandpa, be better protected from bandits, and have Estie closer to your mom, Aaren, since the doctor here can't do anything more for her. I left to help him the next day with the people going back to White Rock."

"So after your dad died, you were pretty much the dad in your family," Aaren said.

"Yeah."

"And then you had to leave them." Aaren looked over at Brock. "It must've been hard."

Brock looked down. He continued walking, retracing the steps we'd taken to get from his house to the barracks. "It wouldn't have been safe to move all our stuff to White Rock in a small group, so my family was going to go with the big group when they headed to the Harvest Festival six months later. But Estie's tumor grew, and it made her legs less stable. Right before they were supposed to leave, she fell. There was swelling, and for a few weeks, they were afraid that if they moved her, they'd do more damage. By the time she was well enough to walk with crutches, they'd missed their chance to leave."

Brock's conversation at the inventions show with the man from Browning popped into my mind. "You found out your family wasn't joining you during the Harvest Festival."

"Yep," Brock said.

"Why didn't you tell us?" Aaren asked.

Brock shrugged. "I wasn't looking for people to feel sorry for me."

We turned onto Brock's street and walked in silence. I thought back through the eight months I'd known him. And about how far he'd been from his family the whole time, and we hadn't even known it.

"I'm sorry," I said as we stepped up to his door. "I hope you get to be with your family again soon."

Brock shrugged and opened the door. Then I couldn't think of anything but the warm house with the warm soup and the warm blankets.

* * *

A pair of hands shook me, but I was so deeply asleep I didn't realize they weren't part of my dream. In the dim light from the fire, I made out the face of Mrs. Sances.

"Time to wake up, Hope. It's a little after three a.m."

I groaned my way to a sitting position, and Mrs. Sances clucked. "I don't think any of you so much as rolled over during the night."

I believed her. Every single muscle in my body ached.

Brenna. She'd been asleep when we got back, and even though Mrs. Sances had assured us she was doing better, I wanted to see for myself.

Brenna was sitting on the couch, holding a mug. "Brock's mom gave me hot cider!"

Relief at her being alive and okay washed over me. She was still pale and weak, though, and it seemed like talking was hard for her, when normally it seemed hard for her to *stop* talking.

Aaren and I both climbed out of our bedrolls and hobbled to her, our muscles too sore to run. "How are you feeling?" Aaren asked as he put a hand on her forehead.

"She's doing okay," Mrs. Sances said. "She woke up a couple hours ago, starving, and ate two bowls of soup. Her body temperature is almost back to normal. She needs sleep, but she wouldn't lie down until you three were awake."

"Is she ready to go?" Aaren asked Mrs. Sances.

"About that." Mrs. Sances pulled Aaren to the side.

"She may look like she's got a little life back in her, but she's far from healed. She goes into the cold right now, and she'll get as bad as she was almost instantly."

Aaren looked at Brenna and bit his lip. "My parents didn't know she snuck out to join us. If I don't bring her home—"

"I know," Mrs. Sances said, her voice softening. "But I bet they'd rather hear she's doing fine in Browning than see her in your arms, knocking on death's door."

Aaren's face fell just like mine did. I hadn't even considered leaving her. But when I'd carried her down the mountain, she had been *so* sick. As much as it hurt my guts, I knew Mrs. Sances was right. It helped that Aaren's mom had been in this house. Surely she'd know Brenna would be well cared for.

Aaren cleared his throat. "Hey, Brenna. I met Brock's sister Estie last night. Did you know she's your age?"

"Yep!" Brenna said. "Mrs. Sances told me."

"I bet she's fun to play with. Want to stay and play with her?"

She smiled and nodded, but I didn't think she realized what that meant. I thought she should. "Brenna," I said, "we need to go back to White Rock right now, but it's still so cold outside. Will you stay here?"

Brenna shivered just thinking about the cold. "Without you?" she asked.

"Yes. And it might be a few weeks before we can come back to get you. But Mrs. Sances will take good care of you and you won't have to be cold."

She looked at me, then Aaren, with big trusting eyes. "I don't want to be cold."

Brock's gaze went to the hallway, with the doors to his siblings' bedrooms. The expression on his face made my heart hurt. It was awful to leave Brenna behind. He had to leave his entire family.

"You could stay." I barely recognized Mrs. Sances's whispered voice. It was full of sadness and hope at the same time, and so much softer than usual.

Brock met her eyes for a few moments before he shook his head. "Grandpa still needs me just as much."

She swallowed hard. "They'll keep you all safe, right? You'll be careful?" We nodded. Then she cleared her throat and clapped her hands together, her gruff kindness returning. "Well, no sense wallowing, especially when breakfast's on the table." She nudged us out of the room, then laid Brenna down in a bed of blankets near the fire.

The kitchen table held plates with pancakes and bacon, and a big pitcher of milk. I shoveled food into my mouth as quickly as I could chew, while Mrs. Sances packed extra food into a bag.

The food probably tasted good, but I ate too fast to tell.

My stomach ached with worries. "We gotta go," I said, gulping down the last of my milk as I stood up.

"They aren't gonna leave without you," Mrs. Sances said as she carried a bag into the front room.

I wasn't so sure. White Rock was the guards' town, too—they were as anxious to get back to help as we were. There was no way they'd wait past four a.m. My feet wouldn't stay still. Neither would my fingers. They drummed the doorknob, aching to turn it. Mrs. Sances finished tying scarves on us, then added item after item to our bags. It had to be 3:30, and we were still standing in Brock's living room.

Finally, Mrs. Sances put the last item in Brock's bag, and we stepped out into the snow-covered streets.

28

Leaving

The sun wouldn't be up for hours, but the light of the moon reflected off the snow and brightened everything. The snow lay piled on top of roofs, trees, fence posts, and roads, but it no longer fell from the sky. In fact, the sky looked calm and clear and innocent. Like it wasn't even capable of creating the blizzard we'd trudged through for so many hours.

I plodded along for the first block with tired, achy muscles; then my body seemed to think that walking nonstop for hours on end was what it was supposed to do now. I got into a rhythm, and the pains faded into the background. After three blocks, the soreness went away enough that we thought we could run. Or maybe it was just panic at the thought of being left behind.

When we rounded the last corner, out of breath, we saw the guard all together, making preparations to leave. Stott gestured and talked with Beckett, his second-in-command, as he walked in our direction. "No Brenna?" he called out. Aaren shook his head. Stott nodded, as if checking one more thing off his mental list, then said, "You're with Travin," and jabbed his thumb toward a group of horses and men behind him.

I couldn't believe how many horses I saw in the moonlight, tromping down the snow. One or two as pack horses I'd expected, but there were probably enough for everyone. All the horses had saddles, even. We sidestepped horse hooves, bustling guard members, and piles of horse poop that steamed in the snow, and made our way to Aaren's brother Travin.

"Where's Brenna?" he asked as we neared him.

Aaren's shoulders sagged. "She was too sick. Think Mom and Dad are going to kill me for leaving her behind?"

Travin put his arm around Aaren's shoulders. "I can guarantee it."

Aaren looked at me in alarm. "He's kidding," I said.

"Yeah. They're much more likely to just send you back out here in the snow to get her."

I turned to see Aaren's darker-haired, older brother Cole as he walked up to us. He patted the neck of the horse closest to Travin. "Nice, huh?"

"Yeah," I said as I stroked the horse's rich, deep brown mane. She reminded me of Arabelle. "Do we get to take these with us?"

Travin grinned. "Yep. Stott met with Browning's captain after you guys left last night. He surprised us with the horses—he said he'll do anything to help White Rock, but I think he just wants us back here quicker. I don't blame him. I'd worry bandits would attack while they didn't have us here, too."

Travin and I climbed onto the brown horse, Aaren and Brock got on a gray one, and Cole walked back into the group to his horse, while Stott and Beckett strode around and made last-minute checks. We moved out less than ten minutes after we got there.

When we passed through the city gates, I couldn't believe what I saw. The mountains that encircled White Rock and the hills that rippled out from it were on my right, but in front of me and to my left lay the flattest ground I'd ever seen, and it went on *forever*. I'd heard this area was covered with houses and roads and schools and stores before the bombs. I tried to picture all of that spread across the flatness. There was so much land! I couldn't imagine there ever being enough buildings to cover that much space. Miles and miles of dark sky stretched everywhere, and only came down to meet the moonlit snow way off in the distance. Everything in White Rock—everything I had spent my entire life looking at—sloped upward. But here things sloped gently downward so far away, it was mesmerizing. It was good that Travin was guiding the horse, because I couldn't take my eyes off the plains.

Except the view of the outside of White Rock was pretty amazing, too. The flat land for miles and miles around made White Rock's crater look massive. No wonder my grandparents and the survivors with them headed toward it when they were looking for a place to call home.

We rode in a long line two horses wide on the main road toward White Rock—the same road we'd take if we were going to enter White Rock through the pass, since it also led to the bridge over White Rock River and the road that circled the crater.

"Have you ever gone anywhere besides Browning?" I asked Cole.

"No."

"Stott has," Travin said. "He's been to both Bergen and Hayes."

"Are there ruins there?" Aaren asked.

"Not that close," Cole said. "You have to go more than two hundred miles away for that. The big cities were mostly wiped out, but I heard there are still a few ruins. Tall buildings used steel framework, though. When the bombs changed the properties of metals, it made them unstable. What's left of the old cities is a death trap— they're nothing like the towns around here. They have their problems; we have ours."

Yeah. I sighed. *We definitely have our own problems.*

As we rode, Travin filled us in on Stott's plan. They were going to leave us at my cousin Carina's house on their way to City Circle; then they'd capture the bandits surrounding the community center and go through multiple doors to overtake the bandits inside. All I could think was how much I wanted to be there when they won. I wanted to make sure my dad was okay. I wanted to see the looks on everyone's faces. I hated the thought of sitting at Carina's house, waiting and waiting for someone to tell us it was over.

Around the Crater

By sunrise, we'd reached the pass—the opening in the crater that lead into White Rock—and I wished we could just go through it instead of having to travel nearly halfway around the mountain. I tilted my head up, amazed at how high the drifts of snow were that filled the pass. Even if I stood on my horse, I wasn't sure I could reach the top of the snow.

A few guards used pickaxes to crack the ice on White Rock River, and we let the horses drink. As soon as they finished, we crossed over the bridge and onto the road that led through the forest around the mountain. If you could call it a road—parts were so narrow we had to go single file. It went around boulders and trees, and over the hills of ripples from the crater. And then back over the hills. And then over them again. I had flashbacks from the night before.

The worst part of the road, though, was when the trees blocked the sun. I was glad I had Travin's warmth behind me, and my horse's warm neck in front of me. But my hands were frozen right through my gloves.

The mountain sat on our right as we circled it. And the roads weren't *all* bad. Part of the way they were even smooth, but the trees were so thick through that part, I couldn't see the amazing plains. I had to be content with watching Brock play with his bale-grabber invention. He said he'd made it for the big bales of cotton they have in Browning, but when he presented it to our class, he told them it was for hay bales. It had a long adjustable rope, with weights on both ends that looked like balls. Aaren rode in front and guided the horse, while Brock rode behind and adjusted the rope as short as it would go, twirled the weights at the ends around and around, then threw it forward. The balls swung to the backside of a tree and wrapped around each other. As their horse reached the tree, Brock would pull it off and go through the process again.

When we stopped to get lunch out of the packs and to stretch our legs, Brock widened his grabber as big as it would go, and he and Aaren each took an end and swung it. The grabber hit a huge boulder and wrapped around it, balls clattering together at the back. He had done a really good job making it. No wonder he won.

"Brock?" I asked. "Do they have competitions for inventions in Browning?"

He glanced at me, then back to the boulder he was aiming at. "Not like they do in White Rock. I don't think people miss the inventions from before the bombs as much. We don't have many books to remind us about them, plus most of the old people who were around before have already died."

It struck me how different life was in Browning. I knew it wasn't as safe, but it hadn't occurred to me that the harder life might have killed off so many. Maybe they didn't care about inventing, but it seemed they had to live in fear of being attacked all the time. I watched Brock swing the bale grabber with Aaren until Stott gave the order to mount up again.

We passed the time predicting what was going on in each of the rooms back at the community center, and what each council member was doing. It helped to distract everyone, but judging by the tense voices of the guards, they were just as anxious as I was. I glanced at the sun to gauge how much time we had before it touched the horizon. Sundown. The time when bad things would happen if we weren't there.

Travin must have been thinking the same thing, because he said, "Two hours. We'll make it."

The sun was dangerously close to the horizon when we finally reached the spot where White Rock River came out of the mountain. We picketed the horses and Stott assigned two men to stay behind with them. He told Clive and Lee to enter first, Beckett to bring up the rear, and the rest of us to keep the person in front of us in sight at all times. After most of the men lit torches, then got on their hands and knees to crawl into an opening just to the left of the river, I went in, with Brock and Aaren right behind me.

"Whoa," Aaren whispered as our eyes adjusted to the torchlight.

The river wasn't as wide here as it was in White Rock—probably not more than forty feet. Inside the cave, a rock ledge a few feet wide ran along the left side of the river, which was a good thing because we needed something to stand on. Ice didn't cover the river inside the mountain. The rock ceiling gradually rose until it was taller than my house, and the cavern was at least fifty feet wide.

The light from the torches bounced off the water in the river and reflected it back onto the walls and ceiling of the cave, so it looked like it was all underwater. A lot of the rock in the cave was white limestone, but all across the ceiling there were big sections that were almost black. It made the ceiling look like a zebra.

"Don't block the way!" Beckett's voice called out from behind me.

I put my back against the wall and shuffled sideways along the stone ledge as fast as I could to catch up.

The ceiling lowered as we traveled into the cave, and the river narrowed and deepened. I moved my schoolbag around to my back and kept my left hand against the wall as we moved forward. In some places the ceiling was so low, I had to crawl. The ground was rough and rocks dug into my knees, ripping through my pants. But at least I didn't have to crawl on my belly like the guard in front of me. The noise of the rushing river was so loud, no one even tried to talk over it.

Most of the way, the ledge was about the same height as the river, but for a terrifying stretch as long as our field at home, it was ten feet above the surface of the water, almost touching the cave ceiling, and barely wide enough to crawl on. I looked down at the water and imagined what would happen if I fell in. The water was so cold, I'd probably freeze instantly; then the river would carry me downstream and shove me under the ice as it exited the mountain. I suppressed a full-body shudder and huddled closer to the wall, focusing on the boots of the guard in front of me.

Once we got past the fall-and-you-die part, the ceiling was tall enough to stand again. I rubbed at my sore knees and hobbled along. After a long stretch, the cave roof lowered to a small opening and I figured it meant more crawling. Instead, I climbed through the opening into a massive cavern. A guard at the opening touched my shoulder, then held a finger to his lips.

I looked around to see why he cared if I was quiet, and that was when I noticed the hole in the ceiling. The hole that led to the mine, and to the bandits guarding it. I moved to the side of the opening, and Brock and Aaren joined me.

Even though I'd followed right behind them, I hadn't looked closely at the frames of the guards' packs. Six of them took off their packs and removed the fabric part that held supplies. The remaining part had two side pieces made of wood that were shaped differently at the top than at the bottom, and three wooden cross pieces, kind of like a ladder. No, *exactly* like a ladder. The six men each slid the top part of their ladder into the bottom part of another ladder, connecting them. When they were done, it was long enough to reach the hole in the rock ceiling. I guess a few of the guards used their downtime in Browning to invent. It was the kind of thing that would likely win an award at the Inventions Contest.

With the ladder in place, Clive and Lee went up to the surface, while we waited. If the bandits saw our guard first, they could warn the other bandits. Or worse, they could shoot Clive and Lee! We barely breathed as we heard a couple of bandits let out startled cries before their bodies hit the ground. Sounds that told us we could go up the ladder and save our town.

30
Battle Plans

All of the guards climbed the ladder before us except Beckett. I stepped from the top rung onto the floor of the mines, and for the first time since the dark-haired bandit shoved my mom, the responsibility that felt like a school-bag full of bricks was lifted from me. The worry about everyone was still there, but we had succeeded! We'd gotten help to White Rock. I practically floated through the tunnel to the large room at the opening.

Aaren stooped next to one of the bandits who lay at the mouth of the cave, and fingered a tiny feathered thing that stuck out of the man's neck. He looked up at Beckett.

"It's a blow dart," Beckett said. "They should be out for a couple of hours"—he nudged the ropes that bound the bandit's feet with his boot—"but they tied them up just in case."

Aaren, Brock, and I put on our snowshoes. I felt bad that the guards didn't have any—the snow went past the knees of most of them. With everyone in town trapped, it wasn't like they had been out shoveling pathways.

The easiest way down the mile and a half to City Circle would have been to follow the tram path nearest the cave entrance. The bandits guarding the community center would have no problem seeing thirty-one of us walk down it, though. Instead, we trudged through the snow behind houses, bushes, and fences.

Stott held up a hand, motioning for us to stop at the edge of the first ring, still half a mile from City Circle and quite a distance from Carina's home. Aaren, Brock, and I would stay there during the fight. He told us all to hide behind a barn while he sent Lee and Aaren's brother Cole ahead as scouts to see how many bandits guarded the outside of the community center.

And then we waited.

Fifteen minutes passed before Lee and Cole returned, out of breath. "They're on their way," Lee said.

"What?" Stott looked back and forth between the two guards. "It isn't sundown yet!"

Lee took a breath. "They're outside the community center, loading food onto horses. The community center's doors are barricaded—probably so they could get away without anyone coming after them. We overheard the one in charge. He said they should tell every town that they killed four of their kids, because it made them hand over the medicine without a fight."

The impact of what Lee said hit me. We had played dead at the edge of the Bomb's Breath when we escaped, but I had told my dad I could go through it without dying. I had assumed that if the bandits told my parents, they would know we were actually okay. I never guessed the bandits would say *they* killed us. So my dad thought I was dead. All my brothers had died before they were even born, and now my mother thought I'd died, too. Aaren's parents thought *two* of their kids were dead. The whole town thought we were dead and didn't know that help was on its way, so they'd handed over the Ameiphus. I took a few steps forward and threw up into a bank of snow.

"How much time?" Stott asked.

Lee shrugged. "Ten minutes, maybe?"

Cole cleared his throat. "That's not all—they have hostages. Williams, Newberry . . ." Cole glanced at Aaren, then back to Stott. "And my mom."

Aaren stiffened, so I reached out and grabbed his hand. I didn't look at him, because I didn't want him to see the panic on my face. I'd never witnessed a battle before—when bandits attacked on our way home from the Planting Festival in Browning, I'd slept in the supply wagon through the whole thing. But it wasn't hard to guess that hostages could accidentally get shot by either side in an attack. I hoped Aaren would never have to experience what I felt when my dad got shot.

The men gathered around Stott, leaving Brock, Aaren, and me blocked by a wall of bodies. But we heard Stott's urgent voice: "Beckett, take your team up to the Kearneys' property. My team, we're at the top of the Romaneks'. Clive, you're on the roof of their house. Lee, I want you on the barn roof. When the hostages are in sight, use the blow darts on whoever's closest to them. No one fires until Clive and Lee give the hostages a chance to run.

"It sounds like they each have a gun, but we don't know if they all have bullets. Assume they do. Stay behind cover until they've wasted as much of their ammo as possible."

Stott took a deep breath, and his next words weren't as rushed. "Our primary objective is to take the medicine back. Shoot to wound only, stay alive, and get them to surrender. I want this orderly and neat. Move out!"

Those with bows adjusted their quivers, the few with guns loaded their ammunition, and Clive and Lee readied their blow darts as they moved away from Stott. Once the crowd cleared and Stott could see us again, it was obvious he'd forgotten about us.

"Hope, Aaren, Brock. Forget Carina's house. It's still too far away. See the Johnsons' house over there?" We all turned to look, even though we knew where it was. It was a bluish-gray home a little downhill and a hundred yards from the tram path. Just far enough from the battle to be safe. "Get there and stay until one of us comes for you. Go. Go!"

We ran as fast as our snowshoes would allow and tried to stay behind fences and bushes. Once we reached the Johnsons' house, we practically fell through the back door and into the kitchen.

"Were we seen?" Brock asked.

Aaren leaned over and put his hands on his knees. "I don't think so."

We stood there a full minute before I was so restless I couldn't stand it. "I have to know what's happening."

"Me too," Aaren said. "My brothers and my mom—"

Brock nodded. "Let's get on the roof."

We slid out the kitchen door, and I looked toward the guards. They must have all gotten into position, because I couldn't see any of them. The grain tram path was just as empty. The air was so clear, I heard the faint murmuring of voices as the bandits came up the trail.

We rushed to the side of the house hidden from the path, took off our snowshoes and tied them to our backs, then climbed up some wooden boxes onto the roof. A thick layer of snow covered everything, so we pushed it off the side and peeked over the edge. I caught a glimpse of the bandits not far from the community center, which meant they were a little less than half a mile from our guard. I counted three horses with them, loaded with food. They were crazy if they thought they'd actually be able to carry that much through the river cave.

The community center was teeny from so far away, but I knew everyone was in there, so I strained to see anyway. Then I noticed two more horses picketed next to the building, knee-deep in snow with no food or water, tethered on short ropes so they couldn't even move around to get warm. I pointed to them. "Can you believe they just left the horses outside? The stables are *right* there. Why do they have to make the horses miserable, too?"

"It'll be over soon," Aaren said, "and we'll take care of them. The ones they're using as pack horses, too."

I sighed. "I know. I just—" I didn't even finish my sentence. They knew what I meant. *I just wish they'd never come.* It wasn't like wishing changed things, though.

I stared at the spot where I would first be able to see the bandits, right where the grain tram lay wedged in a bank of snow at the side of the path. My stomach muscles clenched as the first bandit came into view. This was an actual life-or-death situation. I'd heard of battles plenty of times in history class, but those were with people long dead. People I didn't know. People I didn't care about. With every bandit who stepped into view, I got more and more nervous for our guard. I looked up at the Romaneks' roofs. Clive was on the house roof and Lee on the barn roof, both lying just like we were, their eyes peeking over the tops of the roofs, the rest of their bodies hidden.

When the bandits walked past Holden Newberry's house, I saw their faces. The mean, dark-haired bandit who shoved my mom. Gravel Voice. A teenage bandit from the gym. Shivering Bandit. The three men who chased us to the Bomb's Breath. The shorter, darker-skinned man from the river at the Harvest Festival. A lot of bandits I only vaguely remembered, and the three horses. And of course, Dr. Grenwood, Mr. Newberry, and Mrs. Williams. I didn't count, but it seemed there were about the same number of bandits as our guard.

Then the last one came into view. Mickelson. The second I saw his wavy-haired head rising above the men around him, I imagined the look my parents must have had on their faces when Mickelson told them I was dead.

Then something white caught my eye. We were almost too far away to see it.

"Aaren," I whispered. "On Mickelson's belt. Isn't that your mom's bag?" The bag was about eight inches wide, and about that tall after the top was cinched shut. It was the bag Dr. Grenwood carried at her waist whenever she didn't carry the rest of her medical supplies.

"Yeah," Aaren whispered back. "I bet the Ameiphus is in—"

Aaren was cut off by shouting from the bandits. We held our breath to listen.

"Footprints! There's footprints," one of the men at the front of the line yelled as he gestured toward where we had all stood by the barn.

Since the snow had just fallen, they knew the footprints were from today, but the bandits hadn't gotten close enough for Clive and Lee to reach them with the blow darts. The bandits moved their line into clumps, drew their guns, and aimed them in the direction our guards hid. From the back of the line, Mickelson gave orders I couldn't quite make out, and the men moved up the path and searched for our guard.

When they neared the bushes at the end of the Romaneks' yard, one of the bandits fell to the ground, probably from Clive's blow dart. Mickelson shouted more orders. Some bandits took shots, others ran for cover, and a group of five rushed toward the Kearneys' shed.

The twang of bowstrings, the whiz and thwack of arrows, the crack of gunshots, people shouting, and horses whinnying all carried through the crisp air. Men from both sides moved so much, it was hard to tell who was a bandit and who was our guard. A volley of arrows from our guard took down a few bandits, but people fell to the ground everywhere. By the urgency in Stott's voice, things weren't going as planned. It was chaos. I couldn't tell how many men lying on the ground were from White Rock. I couldn't even tell who was winning.

A movement downhill drew my attention. Mickelson and the other bandit who was always with him were sneaking away from the fight, toward the community center. I gasped. "The horses!" I said as I pointed in their direction. "They're going back down to the horses to escape!"

The guard and the bandits were so caught up in the battle, no one noticed the two men leaving. I yelled as loud as I could, "Stott! Stott!" But the noise from the battle was too loud, and we were too far away. There wasn't a chance in the world he'd hear me.

"If they get to the horses," Brock said, "they can ride up through the woods and take the road to the mines. They'd bypass the fighting and get away."

"Stott!" I screamed. I stood on top of the roof and waved my arms. "Stott!"

Aaren put a hand on my leg. "They'll never get to them in time."

I watched as Mickelson and the other man disappeared behind the tall bushes. Aaren was right. Even if Stott could hear me, the fighting was happening a lot farther up the tram path than where Mickelson and the other bandit were. The guard would never catch them in time. Nothing we had done mattered.

Chasing Bandits

I stood on the roof, feeling more helpless than ever. I'd thought that by going to Browning to get our guard, we'd save our town. But they weren't saved. Mickelson was still getting away with the Ameiphus.

"We have to do something," I said as I slid off the roof into a bank of snow. Aaren and Brock scrambled down after me. We all untied our snowshoes from our backs and put them on.

Brock pulled his bale grabber from my bag and said to Aaren, "I saw a bin of coal by the fireplace for your slingshot."

Aaren took off into the house and called out, "Go! I'll catch up."

I ran as fast as I could toward the tram path; then I

remembered the grain tram. I'd noticed it was lodged in the snow along the path. It would make getting to the community center a lot faster. I told Brock about the tram as we ran. He said, "Get it unstuck. I'll be there in a minute." Then he veered to the left.

When I got to the path, I turned right without even looking toward the sounds of the fight. The battle was the guard's problem. Mine was in front of me, and he was much farther down the path than I'd hoped. I found the tram a couple hundred yards down, grabbed the platform, and gave it a hard tug. It wasn't until Aaren's hands joined mine on the third tug that it came free from the bank and hung from its ropes in the middle of the path.

Brock ran toward us with a coil of rope in his hands that he must have grabbed from a barn. As Brock got closer, I called out, "One . . . two . . . three!" We all jumped onto the platform of the tram at the same time, and the sudden weight launched it down the path.

The wind rushed past as we sped along, snow billowing out behind us. I sat with my legs hanging over the short wall in the front so my snowshoes were out of the way, and put my hands on the brakes. We needed speed to catch up, but I didn't want to hit the ending pole, either.

The bandits pounded through the snow ahead of us, nearing the horses. The sounds of the battle behind us and their running must have covered the sounds of the tram, because they didn't notice us. We'd been on the path for less than a minute and were already two-thirds of the way down. I leaned forward to make us go even faster.

Several hundred yards ahead, the horses stood to the left of the tram path, in the open space just before the ditch and the shops that circled the community center. If we went as far as the tram would go, it would take us past the horses, the ditch, and the buildings and land us right on the road. I set my sights on the buildings, because nothing else would block us from a bullet. It meant we'd pass by Mickelson and the other bandit, but I hoped we'd go by so fast they couldn't get us.

As we neared the last upright post before the horses, I positioned my feet on the brakes, but it didn't matter. The rope for the last section wasn't tight. The tram sagged and we went slower and slower until it lodged itself in the snow. Unfortunately, the bandit with Mickelson chose that moment to glance back.

"Hey!" the man yelled, and by the look of surprise on Mickelson's face when he turned, I guessed he actually thought we had died. We jumped off the tram and ran as fast as we could toward the buildings. We had snowshoes, but they had longer legs. We could tell we'd never make it to the buildings, so as soon as we reached the ditch, we dove into it.

It blocked us from them, but we knew it wouldn't save us for long.

"The guy with Mickelson used all his bullets before they left the fight," Brock said. "I didn't see Mickelson, though."

Aaren pulled his slingshot out of his bag as we hunched down in the ditch. "I did. He didn't fire a single shot."

I poked my head up, then ducked just as quickly when I saw the bandits running toward us, less than twenty-five feet away. "There's no way he gave all the bullets to his men," I said. "He has some."

Brock uncoiled his bale grabber and shortened it as much as it would go, while Aaren gave me his schoolbag of coal and asked me to keep handing him one piece at a time. He stood up and shot piece after piece of coal with his slingshot, faster than I'd ever seen him shoot. I could barely keep up with him. Each shot made the two bandits move away from each other.

Mickelson stayed back, but the other man inched closer, trying to reach us. Brock swung the ends of his bale grabber around and around while I kept handing coal to Aaren.

"Now," Aaren said, his lips barely moving.

Brock stood up and flung his bale grabber toward the man. The grabber wrapped around his legs, and the man fell to the ground. He cursed as he struggled to free himself.

"Cover me," Brock said as he grabbed the rope from the ground and ran to the man.

I hesitated, not knowing if I should run forward to help Brock tie up the bandit or continue handing coal to Aaren so he could keep Mickelson away from Brock.

Mickelson stood close enough that I saw a vein in his forehead bulge as he ground his teeth. He had always been so calm and in control. I wasn't sure which scared me worse—the Purposeful Mickelson, or this Out-of-Control Mickelson.

I should have ducked. I should have run. I should have hid. *Something*. Instead, I froze like I had stone legs as Mickelson raised his gun and aimed it right at me.

32 Trick

Maybe my entire body turned to stone, because I couldn't breathe. Or hear the yelling from Brock and Aaren. I just stared into Mickelson's eyes, petrified.

And then I heard a loud *crack!* and Mickelson's hand flew to the side. His gun landed in the snow half a dozen feet from where he stood, and I was no longer frozen like a statue. I whirled to face Aaren. He stood, slingshot in hand, a look of calm concentration on his face, the same look he got when he helped his mom treat someone who was badly injured. He loaded another piece of coal into his slingshot.

Mickelson grabbed his hurt hand and lunged for the gun. Before he got to it, Aaren fired a second shot and hit him in the shoulder. Mickelson threw a look of barely contained fury in Aaren's direction; then the calm, controlled Mickelson returned.

He stared at Brock and the other bandit, then at Aaren and me, then he turned. Away from the gun, away from us. Like we didn't matter at all.

"He doesn't have to beat us," I breathed. "He just has to leave with the Ameiphus and he wins."

As the words came out of my mouth, Mickelson took off running toward the horses, leaving the other bandit behind. He untied Arabelle's reins, swung onto her back, and galloped toward the woods.

We scrambled out of the ditch, and Aaren ran to help hold down the bandit Brock was struggling to tie up.

My breath came fast. "I have to go after Mickelson. I have to get the Ameiphus." I paused long enough to see the worried look on Aaren's face, the one that said he didn't want me to go but knew I would anyway, and to be careful. He nodded once before he turned away, and I ran for Chance.

I couldn't believe Mickelson took Arabelle and left me Chance. *Chance,* of all horses! He was saddled—that was something, at least. I flung off my snowshoes, untied him, climbed into the saddle, and jabbed my heels into his sides.

The wind bit my face and I bounced up and down as Chance galloped through the snow toward Mickelson.

Most of the time I couldn't see Mickelson as he went around houses, barns, and fences on his way through the first ring. At least with Chance, I didn't have to go around low fences—he'd jump right over them . . . some of the time. He jumped the first two fences, but at the third he stopped. His stubbornness could have ended it all for me. The only thing Chance hated more than doing what he was supposed to, though, was being saddled and picketed. It made him want to run.

It took me nearly a mile to catch up to Mickelson at the end of the second ring, half a mile into the woods. I was close enough to see the white bag of Ameiphus tied to his belt. If I didn't get it before Mickelson reached the end of the third ring, he could turn left on the road and go straight to the mines. I urged Chance closer so I could grab it.

The sound of his hooves pounding through the snow into the frozen ground felt as loud as my heartbeat as I got closer and closer. My outstretched hand was a foot away from the bag when Mickelson kicked at Chance's shoulder and made him turn away. I got Chance to edge near them a second time, and Mickelson kicked Chance again.

Chance's body was too big a target—I had to give Mickelson a smaller one. My mind went back to all the times I had watched Cass stunt-ride on Arabelle. I thought of the tricks they did and cursed again the fact that Mickelson rode Arabelle and I got Chance. The best trick was one where Cass hung by a hand on the pommel and one foot in a stirrup, and lay with her back pressed against the side of her horse. That could put me lower, and if I stretched, only Chance's head would be within Mickelson's reach. I hoped it was as easy as Cass made it look, because it was my only idea.

Cass had worked with Arabelle for weeks before they'd succeeded with the trick. At first, whenever Cass swung over her side, Arabelle would assume she'd fallen off and stop dead in her tracks. Eventually Arabelle learned to trust Cass. But it had always been my experience with riding Chance that he didn't care even a little bit if his rider fell off.

Mickelson rode on my left, so I grabbed the pommel tightly with my left hand, planted my left foot in the stirrup, and then threw my body off the left side of the horse. As my back hit Chance's side, I got the wind knocked out of me and my hand was nearly pulled off the pommel, but I did it. I was lying flat against Chance's side. With my head against his neck, I imagined the bag in my hand as I reached forward as far as I could to grab it. I was within inches when Chance decided he was more interested in something off to the right than he was in Mickelson and slowed way down.

Sometimes I hated that horse.

I grabbed the cheek piece of his bridle with my free

arm and jabbed him in the hindquarter with my free foot, aiming his head toward Mickelson. Chance closed the gap between us. I didn't let go of his bridle until his head was almost to Mickelson's waist. I gave Chance another nudge in the hindquarter. When he pulled forward, I let go of his bridle, then reached out and ripped the bag from Mickelson's belt just as Mickelson reached out and shoved Chance's head to the side.

Chance turned to the right and slowed to a walk, but not before I held the little white bag in my hand. The bag worth invasions and battles and gunshots and lives.

Mickelson jerked Arabelle to a stop and yanked her head toward me. He swore so loudly it startled Chance, making him almost fall when my unbalanced weight and his sidestep made his hoof hit a toppled tree hidden under the snow. As soon as he regained his footing, he took off running. My left arm shook with exhaustion, but I somehow managed to pull myself back into the saddle and shove the Ameiphus inside my schoolbag.

Mickelson rode after us, looking like he wanted to fling me off my horse even more than Chance wanted to be rid of me. Actually, he looked like he wanted to do something worse than fling me off. I jabbed Chance with my heels and yelled, "Go, go, go!"

I knew I needed a plan, but everything happened so fast.

The Bomb's Breath! It was almost a mile away, but on horses it wouldn't take long. If I took the Ameiphus through the Bomb's Breath, Mickelson wouldn't be able to get it.

There wasn't a path through the woods, so we galloped around trees and over bushes and logs. Chance took every opportunity to sideswipe trees, which whipped twigs at my face and arms and scraped my legs on the trunks. Once I had to duck when he ran under a low-hanging branch as he tried to knock me off his back. To his annoyance, I managed to stay on.

Maybe Chance hadn't been ridden lately. Maybe he'd been tethered too long. Maybe he was more impatient than normal. For whatever reason, he wanted to run fast, which worked for me. So many things about him frustrated me, and so I never really appreciated his speed. For every step Chance took, I heard Arabelle's hooves crunch through the snow right behind us.

I saw the warning fences before we broke out of the woods. We jumped over the last clump of bushes and galloped across the road. *Just one leap over the warning fence,* I told myself, *then another hundred feet or so and I can jump off Chance and run through the Bomb's Breath.*

And then Chance stopped right in the middle of the road so quickly that my forward momentum flung me off him, and I landed in the snow on my stomach.

Threats

Chance had just plain stopped. He hadn't slowed or looked skittish; he just stopped. I glared at him for half a second before Arabelle and Mickelson jumped over the last cluster of bushes at the edge of the woods; then I scrambled to my feet and bolted over the warning fence.

I pushed through the knee-deep snow as fast as I could, waving my arms above me to feel for the dense air. Aaren and I had sky jumped in the Bomb's Breath not too far from here—there was a spot to my left where the landscape was like a playground—but with everything covered in snow, I didn't have a good sense of landmarks. I had no idea where the Bomb's Breath started.

Arabelle's hoofbeats pounded behind me. Of course

she had jumped the fence. She was Arabelle. I stretched up once more, hoping I'd found the Bomb's Breath, but I wasn't close enough. Mickelson was almost on me.

I took the sack of Ameiphus from my schoolbag right as Arabelle caught up to me. Mickelson reached down and grabbed my hair. "Give it to me," he growled.

I hucked the bag as high and as far as I could manage. With my hair in Mickelson's hand, I had to squirm to keep my eyes on it, but I breathed a sigh of relief when its descent slowed, because that meant it made it into the Bomb's Breath before it landed in the snow.

Mickelson must have known enough about the Bomb's Breath to recognize the bag had fallen there, because he instantly understood what had happened. He slid off Arabelle and yanked my hair so hard, I fell flat on my back in the snow. The shock froze me in place. I didn't even reach up to rub my pained scalp.

Mickelson took a step to stand over me. "Get it." His voice came out like it was barely contained inside a bomb, about to explode.

I let out a hysterical squeak as I realized I should have ridden toward our guard when I got the Ameiphus instead of going to the Bomb's Breath, because then I'd have had help. As it was, I lay there all alone in the cold snow and couldn't think what to do. I could only think of the way the vein on Mickelson's forehead pulsed, and the way his warm breath came out of his nostrils in puffs, making little clouds in the cold air. Like a picture I saw once of an angry bull.

The sun had just begun to set, filling a huge swath of the sky with a million shades of pink. It reflected off the snow and colored everything, like the air itself had an eerie, unreal shade.

Mickelson took several long breaths before he spoke. "I don't need to remind you that your entire town is trapped in the community center. Or that your guard is busy with my men. Your horse is long gone. If you don't give me the Ameiphus, I will ride down to the community center and throw a torch inside. My men have already boarded the doors, so they won't be able to escape. The fire will kill everyone. There'd be no one to stop me."

He pulled me to a standing position as if I weighed nothing. "Get the Ameiphus now. If you value the life of your town, your friends, your parents, you'll find a way to throw it to me, even if it's with your dying breath."

I'd never been so scared in all my life. Not when the bandits first came to the community center, not when they chased us, not when the snowstorm was at its worst, not even when I saw the fighting. Every part of me shook with fear. My hands, my legs, my chin, my stomach, my heart.

By the look on his face, I knew he'd kill all of us if I didn't get him the Ameiphus.

His eyes drilled into mine, angry and determined and demanding. I nodded and walked toward the Bomb's Breath. I had no other choice. I waved my arms until I found the start of the pressurized air, then took a deep breath and stepped into it.

34
Choices

I couldn't find the bag of Ameiphus. My head was bent back when I threw it, but I thought I knew where it landed. I pushed my hands into the snow and felt all around until I couldn't hold my breath another second, then I ran up the mountain to get out of the Bomb's Breath. Over and over, and I still couldn't find it.

With every second, Mickelson's anger grew, and I worried more and more what would happen if I couldn't find the bag. Maybe one of my million footprints had buried it completely. When I ran back above the Bomb's Breath again, I thought about how finding a white bag hidden in white snow was much worse than finding a needle in a haystack.

Then I saw a shadow fifteen feet to the left of where I'd

been searching. A shadow from a hole in the snow, where the sunset hit one side differently.

I ran to the shadow. The bag had gone in at an angle and was completely hidden. I almost cried in relief when my fingers closed around the sack. I ran up the mountainside to get out of the Bomb's Breath and took a shaky breath. My hands held the sack that represented the lives of people I cared about. My dad's life. Mr. Hudson's life. Melina's life. The lives of everyone who would get Shadel's Sickness or some other bad infection.

I couldn't hand it to Mickelson. I couldn't watch person after person die because of my decision. But did I have a choice? I could give it to him, and people would die. Or I could keep it, and he'd set the community center on fire and people would die.

I couldn't win.

"Bring it to me now," Mickelson said. I didn't move, not even to breathe. He watched me for a long while, then said, "Your dad's the one I shot, right?" His voice was calm and controlled again.

I could barely nod.

"Tell you what. I'll give you a dose of the Ameiphus for your dad. You'll save him. I'll even give you a dose for that other man."

"Mr. Hudson?"

Mickelson nodded. "The girl, too. Give it to me, and I

won't set the community center on fire. Not only will you save your dad, but you'll save your whole town. You'll go back a hero."

We stared at each other for a long minute. Then he spoke again. "You don't have to worry whether I'll hold up my end of the bargain. Take out three doses, then toss the bag to me." He nodded to the left. "I'll go that way to the mines, away from everyone. Your town will carry you home on their shoulders, singing your praises."

The phrases I'd chanted on the mountain—*Save Brenna, save my dad, save White Rock*—echoed in my thoughts. This was the only way to win. It wasn't a perfect option, but it was definitely the least bad one.

Except, I realized, it didn't *really* save my town. It was just three doses of Ameiphus better than if I'd never left to get the guard in the first place. And the battle I'd witnessed from the Johnsons' rooftop would be for nothing. The men I'd seen lying on the ground in the snow would be for nothing.

You're more of a leader than you realize. My dad's voice popped into my head, which was weird, since there wasn't anyone around for me to lead. Then my mom's voice: *You find yourself in any situation and instantly know what to do.*

I froze. They were right. People followed me, just like they followed my dad. Not because they thought I was good at inventing—they followed because they knew I'd figure out what to do. If we were bored, I'd figure out how to have fun. If we were lost or in trouble, even if it happened because of how I'd helped us have fun, I'd find a way out of it.

So I should be able to find my way out of this, too.

I looked down at the bag in my hands. Shadel's Sickness didn't exist before the bombs, and neither did Ameiphus. They came together—a great weakness and a great strength. Like they were balancing each other out. Standing there, I realized that I'd been trying to contribute to my town by using my biggest weakness, just because it was how everyone else contributed. I should have been using my biggest strength.

I faced Mickelson with a determination I'd never felt before. I studied his face, trying to figure out what went on in his head, while he studied my face back. My gut told me it was more important to him to get the Ameiphus than to light the community center on fire. If I ran on my side of the Bomb's Breath toward our guard, it might take a couple of hours to reach them, but I guessed Mickelson would follow just below the Bomb's Breath, matching every step I took. If I got lucky, in an hour or so when it was completely dark, I'd lose him.

And that was when Mickelson took a deep breath and stepped right into the Bomb's Breath.

Jump

Nobody went through the Bomb's Breath but Aaren, Brock, Brenna, and me. *Nobody.* Mickelson tromped through it with disbelief and anxiety on his face that pretty much matched mine. When he hiked as high as me, he took a few big gasps of air and looked like he couldn't believe he was still alive.

I pushed aside my shock and tried to think. Even with the snow, I knew the area well enough. Up ahead, the ground split into a crevice right before the terrain really got rough. The crevice wasn't more than eight feet deep and the other side was just close enough to grab when you jumped—but to go around it, you had to hike several hundred yards. I ran, building speed as I neared a huge pine tree next to the crevice that kept the ground around it free of snow.

At the edge, I planted my foot and leapt as far across the opening as I could. My body smacked into the wall of the crevice as I caught the top of it with my hands. It took all my strength to pull myself up without footholds. I knew Mickelson would follow, and I hoped it was a lot harder for him to lift a man-sized body. I hoisted my legs onto the ground just in time to see Mickelson take a running jump across the crevice and land on his feet on my side.

I hadn't planned for his longer legs! I scrambled to my feet and ran, taking the only good path. Cliffs rose on my right, and large boulders filled almost every space of the sloping mountainside leading to a drop-off on my left. I cringed when I heard Mickelson's long string of swear-words and threats behind me. He was following me too well. I had to leave the path.

I pushed my hands into the snow on one of the boulders, swung my feet over it, and landed below the path on another boulder. Tons of rocks of every size ran between the path and the ledge. I skipped from boulder to boulder. It felt like I was getting away, but in reality, Mickelson and his constant threats were close behind me.

He leapt and landed on a rock so close he could almost

reach me. He held my eyes as he panted, a look of victory on his face. "You can't outrun me," he said.

He was right.

The realization hit me like a boulder slamming into my stomach. I wasn't going to win. No matter what I did, he got closer. My plan to lose him or go where he couldn't had failed.

That meant I had two options. I could leap across a couple more boulders before Mickelson grabbed me, or I could jump off the ledge. I looked over the side and gulped. The cliff was higher than anything I'd jumped off without the Bomb's Breath to catch me.

But if I couldn't outrun Mickelson, my only choice was to outjump him.

And I actually, truly, had science on my side. A year ago, Mrs. Romanek had taught us about the Law of Conservation of Energy, which said energy couldn't be destroyed, only transferred. Normally, I tuned out science without even trying to, but that lesson felt made for me. In a *Pay attention, Hope—this is how you'll be able to jump from higher distances without getting hurt* kind of way. So I paid attention and found out that if I tucked and rolled as I landed, the force of the fall wouldn't go squarely to my legs—it would be displaced through the roll. I tried it dozens of times in the week after the lesson. This was much higher than I'd ever tried, but at least I had the snow as a cushion.

Even with the extra science knowledge and practice, the height *still* scared me, which meant there was no way Mickelson would jump.

I stepped to the edge, filled my lungs with air, and jumped off the cliff, trying not to freak out that the Bomb's Breath wasn't going to slow my fall. I concentrated on where I'd place my hands and legs, and pictured what I was going to do when I landed, while the wind rushed past me. I hit the ground in a roll, and what air I had left was knocked out of me. With my forward momentum, I rolled into a standing position and coughed a few heaving breaths. As I brushed the snow off, I looked at the top of the cliff. It was so high, I couldn't believe I'd actually jumped!

Mickelson stood silhouetted at the cliff's edge, the sunset glowing a brilliant pink and orange behind him. His posture showed how haggard he was. Still, I could tell he was considering jumping. Chances were he'd chicken out, but I glanced downhill for an escape route anyway.

A huge clump of trees grew directly above a spot that everyone called the Dimple. You could see it from almost anywhere in White Rock. The woods looked like a man's beard, the group of trees to my left looked like the mustache, and a pit in the ground below it, right in the middle of the Bomb's Breath, looked like a dimple on his cheek. If Mickelson jumped, that was where I'd go. I waited to see if he'd actually do it.

He did. And his jump was beautiful. He soared through the air with his arms slightly windmilling, the sunset behind him, his curly hair blown back by the wind as it rushed past him. By the time he neared the ground, his body was perfectly upright. He landed straight down on his feet, but he didn't tuck and roll. The force propelled him forward, knocking him facedown. If it wasn't for the snow, he'd have broken both legs for sure.

Mickelson staggered to a standing position, looking like everything hurt, and took a step toward me.

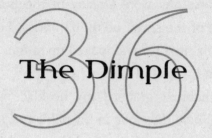

The Dimple

I backed in the direction of the trees above the Dimple, keeping my eyes on Mickelson. He took careful steps toward me until I stopped behind two tree trunks about three feet apart, only a couple of feet uphill from the Dimple.

The lowest branch on either tree was eight feet off the ground. I put one foot on one tree trunk, then jumped my second foot onto the second trunk, with one hand on each tree. I alternated my weight between my feet as I scaled up the trees. When I was high enough, I pushed off one trunk and swung onto a branch of the other, a nice sturdy branch that stuck straight out. As I hunched down on it, I saw exactly what I'd hoped to see—Mickelson standing between me and the Dimple. I knew from playing here and almost falling from that drop-off, it was deep enough that the bottom had normal air and the Bomb's Breath covered the top like a lid.

Mickelson's feet were already in the Bomb's Breath, but because of the snow, he didn't notice. He shifted his weight off his hurt leg and looked up at me, trying to figure out what I was doing.

Out of habit, I grabbed my necklace as I watched Mickelson. I held the stone in my palm and ran my finger and thumb down the chain. At that second, I realized the pendant and the chain *did* go together. There were parts of me that were rough, and parts that were polished. There were things I was great at and things I stank at. Everything together made up me. Imperfect me, but capable me. Definitely find-a-way-out-of-this-mess me.

And right now, I could get out of this mess if I could get Mickelson trapped in the Dimple. If I could swing down from the branch I crouched on, I could use my feet to push him in.

"I don't want you to die," I said.

"Funny. The longer you keep that bag of Ameiphus, the more I want you to die." He looked up at me with his controlled, confident expression. "You can't stay up there all day. The second you come down, I'm going to throw you off that cliff." He nodded toward his left. "The Ameiphus won't be so hard to take from you when you're lying broken at the bottom. You're trapped. You've got nowhere to run. It's over. The only way to save yourself is to drop the Ameiphus to me now."

"I still don't want you to die," I repeated. "So take a big breath and hold it, okay?"

He tilted his head to the side and crinkled his forehead.

"Now!" I yelled. I reached down and grabbed the branch with my hands, then threw my feet behind me. As I held on to the branch, my legs went under the tree, and I pulled my feet together as they swung toward Mickelson. I aimed right for his chest. He gasped; then my feet hit him with enough force that he flew backward. The jerk of the hit pulled my hands off the branch, and I dropped flat on my back in the snow as he tumbled and fell right into the Dimple.

I got up and ran to the edge of the Bomb's Breath. Mickelson had landed in the pit on his back. I let out a huge breath that was equal parts exhaustion, relief, and pure joy. Mickelson was trapped.

He jumped to his feet, even though the motion looked painful, and attempted to scramble up the walls of the pit.

"Don't!" I shouted. "If you climb up, you'll be in the Bomb's Breath, and you'll die."

He froze. And for the first time since he stepped through the Bomb's Breath, he was speechless.

"Stay there," I said. "I'll get people to haul you up with a rope."

I reached into my schoolbag as I walked away from him, pulled out the sack of Ameiphus, and grinned. It was safe. I opened it, just to see the little white pills.

Except they were no longer white.

Most of the pills in the bag had changed to the blue of the sky on a summer's day. I just stared at them, baffled. These pills were always white. I didn't know what could have changed them.

My eyes flashed to the Bomb's Breath. That was the one thing different with these pills than every other Ameiphus pill I'd seen. They had gone through the Bomb's Breath.

Some of the pills were still mostly white—probably the ones that had been in the middle of the sack while it sat in the snow, waiting for me to find it. I knelt down and felt around for the start of the dense air. With several of the ones that were white in the palm of my hand, and with my breath quivering, I moved them into the air of the Bomb's Breath.

I watched with fascination as they changed from white to a faint blue, then to a light blue, and finally to a brilliant sky blue. *What was going on? Were they ruined?* I stared at them, biting my lip and wondering what the change meant before returning the pills to their sack.

With my schoolbag over my shoulders again and the

Ameiphus safe inside, I backed up quite a bit, ran as fast as I could, and leapt into the air just before I reached the Bomb's Breath. I wasn't high above it, so I took a deep breath the moment my feet left the ground. My forward momentum shot me past the Dimple, and I put my arms and legs straight out. The Bomb's Breath wouldn't hold me forever, but for a moment I didn't think about that. I just enjoyed the weightlessness. I had the Ameiphus. My town was safe. As impossible as it seemed, I had actually won.

I was flying.

I curled into a ball, feet down, as I neared the bottom of the Bomb's Breath, then dropped out of it and landed with a thump in the snow. The only sound I heard was my own breath as it made frozen clouds in front of my face, then the sound of Arabelle's snort from somewhere in the trees.

She galloped toward me from the edge of the woods and nuzzled into my shoulder. I laid my cheek on her forehead and patted her jaw. "Thanks for waiting for me, Arabelle."

I climbed into her saddle, wrapped my arms around her neck, and together we rode toward City Circle.

37

Ameiphus

Arabelle must have sensed my impatience to get to my family, because she rode in the straightest line possible to City Circle, jumping over fences, bushes, ditches, and the occasional doghouse. After only a few minutes, I saw the rooftop of the community center.

When Arabelle and I passed between the last two merchant shops, I saw a long stream of people trudging up the tram path to help our guard. I leapt off Arabelle and ran through a demolished door of the community center, heading straight to the gym. They must have just broken free, because everything was chaotic.

No one noticed me slip into the room, which I was grateful for. All I wanted was my parents. I searched the crowd, but I couldn't see them anywhere. Then someone grabbed my arm. I turned to see Mrs. Davies.

"Hope! You're alive!" she said. Then her face crinkled into a concerned expression. "Your parents are in the clinic. Hurry!"

Fear grabbed my heart. I pushed through the crowd and into the hallway, then burst through the clinic doors into a room almost as crowded as the gym. All three beds were occupied, with worried family members on and around them, but my eyes could only focus on my parents.

My dad was asleep in one of the beds, looking pained, his skin not even close to the right color. My mom was sitting on the edge of the bed, her eyes red and puffy. The moment she saw me, she jumped up and hugged me tight. I melted into her arms. After a moment, she whispered, "I knew you weren't dead."

I bent down and wrapped my arms around my dad, pressing my cheek into the stubble on his cheek. His skin burned against mine. I looked to my mom in alarm.

"The antibiotic cream wasn't enough," she whispered. "The infection spread. When people see him, it's like they know he's going to die." She sniffed and wiped away a tear. "When we decided to hand the Ameiphus over to Mickelson, everyone gave up on your dad." She paused and met my eyes. "But I knew you wouldn't."

I pulled Dr. Grenwood's sack full of the medicine from my bag, and my mom's breath caught at the sight of it. When I tipped a blue pill into my hand, she gave me a puzzled look. "It's all right," I said. "I think."

We gently shook my dad's shoulders, and his eyes fluttered open. "Hope?" he said with confused eyes.

"It's me," I said. "I'm okay. I need you to take this." I held the pill to his lips. He opened his mouth and my mom gave him a drink of water. His eyes closed again, and he was asleep instantly.

"You did good," Brock said behind me.

I turned and smiled. "Thanks. So did you guys."

"The Ameiphus is blue?" Aaren asked.

I held the bag out to him. "Yep. Something happened when they went through the Bomb's Breath."

Aaren's eyes flicked back and forth, and he got his focused-on-science look while his mind worked through the details of what must have happened when the pills were exposed to the Bomb's Breath. "Come on," he said. "Let's get some to Mr. Hudson and Melina."

Mr. Hudson's wife and sons wore faces full of relief. Mr. Hudson looked as bad as my dad. Worse, if you counted the blotchy spots all over his skin. Aaren put his arm under Mr. Hudson's shoulders to lift him up a bit, then put one of the pills in his mouth and gave him a drink. Brock took a pill to Melina in the third bed. She was so little—only a year or two older than Brenna. She didn't have the blotchy skin yet. Maybe with the medicine, she wouldn't get as bad as Mr. Hudson was.

When Dr. Grenwood returned to the community center from her stint as a hostage, we heard the happy reunion in the hallway. Aaren ran out to join them. A moment later, his mom walked into the clinic with Aaren's dad's arm around her shoulders and Aaren and his siblings surrounding her. I could tell that the past few days had been even worse for her than for us. When she saw me with the bag of Ameiphus, the look on her face made our entire trip worth it. I hoped she would forgive us for leaving her daughter behind in Browning.

A group of people rounded up all the bandits, while Dr. Grenwood and Aaren moved between the three patients in the clinic and the chaos of the celebration and the nine wounded guards in the gym. The whole time, I sat with my mom in a bubble of calm on my dad's bed.

"Before the fever got bad," she said, "your dad decided he's going to run for council head."

I looked at my dad's face, then at my mom's. "What? How?" Nothing had changed. I wasn't any better at inventing.

She reached out and ran her hand down my hair. "I think you reminded us both how to be strong."

I smiled. "I did?"

She nodded. "Most of the town has been begging him to run, and I told him I support him one hundred percent. I think we're both finally ready."

I looked up at her in shock. "It wasn't me?" My mom gave me a confused look. I swallowed my own confusion and searched her eyes for the truth. "*I'm* not the reason he wouldn't run? Because I'm such an embarrassment?"

"Hope." Her voice was so sad, like maybe her heart hurt. "You've *never* embarrassed us."

My mom put her arm around me. I leaned into her shoulder, finally relaxing, and fell asleep.

After two hours, my dad's fever broke and he woke up. I was awake and skimming my fingertips across his big, thick fingers when I heard his voice, sounding more like a croak.

"You're alive."

I looked at his face, which was much more normal-colored than it had been, and smiled. "You too."

He squeezed my hand. "Course we are. I told you— you're the most capable girl I know, Hope." He paused a moment and smiled. "You do know you're grounded, right?"

I squeezed his hand back and grinned. "Yep, I know."

Winter Festival

I shivered in the cavern below the hole in the mine floor as I waited with Brock, Aaren, and Aaren's family. I linked my arms in Aaren's and Brock's, hoping to share some of their warmth. "What's taking them so long?" I asked.

I knew Aaren was as anxious as I was. It had been a long three weeks since we'd last seen Brenna. And two days since Aaren's dad, his brother Cole, and a couple of guards left for Browning to get her and bring her back.

Aaren's little brothers, James, Quin, and Nick, ran to where the cave room and river narrowed to a tunnel. Nick tilted his ear toward the opening and pointed. "I hear voices!"

Everyone strained to hear Brenna's chattering from the tunnel opening. I couldn't believe how much I had missed that voice! A few minutes later, Beckett crawled through the tunnel into the cave room, followed by Brenna, Mr. Grenwood, Cole, and Clive.

They were immediately surrounded, and I joined the reunion like it was my family. Brenna breathlessly told us about her trip home and her stay at Brock's house with her new best friend, Estie. She looked like she might explode if she didn't tell all three weeks' worth of news soon.

"Oh! Oh!" Brenna said. "I didn't tell you the best part! They're all going to move here the second the snow melts in the tunnel. So you'll get your family, Brock, and I'll get Estie!"

I wondered if Brock would shout for joy or jump up and down, but what I saw on his face was even better. His look of a million worries had come back as soon as we left Browning, but when Brenna gave him the news, all that lifted and he smiled bigger than I'd ever seen him smile. Until Brenna almost knocked him over when she plowed into him with a hug.

"Come on," Mr. Grenwood said as he lifted Brenna onto the ladder leading up to the mines. "Let's talk on the way. I'm sure the sledding races are over, but there's still a lot of Winter Festival fun to be had."

We usually held the Winter Festival in the gym at the community center, but our town had spent too much time in the gym lately. Everyone agreed that having the Winter

Festival outside where it actually felt like winter was the best thing anyway. One of the city office rooms in the community center had been turned into a temporary jail until a real one could be built. It held six of Mickelson's men, so that helped make the decision, too.

By the time guards reached the woods to pull Mickelson out of the Dimple, he was gone, and he hadn't been seen again. Until the mine workers could seal the hole in the mine floor, a few of our guards watched it constantly so he couldn't come back.

As we stepped out of the cave, the last bit of sun dipped behind the top of the mountain, and we followed the river by the light of the sunset. In the distance, the smoke from the fires rose into the sky. If I squinted, I could see past the fires to the place where we'd held the remembrance ceremony just over two weeks ago for the three guards who died in the battle with the bandits. I closed my eyes and thanked them again for saving everyone.

The closer we got to the party, the louder the voices of everyone in town became, the darker the skies got, and the more my teeth chattered.

When we rounded the last bend in the river, the Winter Festival was in sight. Dozens of fires burned in a massive circle, with a circle of tables inside that, and the performance platform right in the middle. All the tables that had held the inventions at the Harvest Festival were ready for our feast. The smells drifted along the air like happiness itself. We raced between two of the fires to join our town in the celebration, and a group formed around Brenna, Cole, Dr. Grenwood, Clive, and Beckett.

My parents waved me over, and I ran to them.

"I see Brenna made it back safely," my dad said.

"Yep." I glanced at Brenna and the others.

"Then it's time to get this party started." There hadn't been an official vote yet to see if my dad was the new council head, but everyone except Mr. Newberry acted like he was. My dad walked to the center of the platform, grabbed the bullhorn, and said the words the council head says every year: "Let the feast begin!"

Once everyone finished eating, we found a spot in front of the performance platform to sit and watch the storytellers, and I snuggled up next to Aaren, Brock, and Brenna. A few people placed torches around the obelisk in the center of the platform so we could see.

A hush came over the crowd as Mr. Hudson walked onto the platform. I nudged Aaren. "Why is he up there?"

Aaren shrugged.

I couldn't believe how healthy Mr. Hudson looked! He'd come down with Shadel's only three weeks ago. Even with Ameiphus, he should have been in bed for another three weeks, yet here he was, looking normal. I heard that Melina had healed even more quickly.

"I consider it quite a privilege to be up here tonight," Mr. Hudson said. "The Winter Festival is a celebration of life—of our ability to make it through the coldest, darkest times. I think we can agree that as a town, we've recently made it through some pretty cold, dark times."

Chills ran down my back. After all we had been through, this Winter Festival felt different from any other one I'd been to. And it wasn't just because we were outside. I think it was because as a town, we felt different.

"I know many of you have been shocked at how quickly I made it through my own cold, dark time." Mr. Hudson glanced upward for a moment. "Although the Bomb's Breath is invisible and deadly, it protects us. It makes our town stronger. And now Dr. Grenwood has confirmed that the chemical change that occurred when the medicine was exposed to the air of the Bomb's Breath also made the Ameiphus stronger."

The crowd sat in silent awe as we processed the news. Dr. Grenwood had said that since Shadel's Sickness was a side effect of the green bombs, the cure would be as well. It made sense that the thing that made the medicine stronger would be a side effect of the green bombs, too.

Mr. Hudson continued. "Many of us have been

personally touched by the loss of a loved one who died because of the Bomb's Breath. We have great reason to fear it. Yet we live in a unique situation in White Rock. We're the only location within hundreds of miles with not only the optimal conditions for growing Ameiphus, but with an altitude high enough to access the Bomb's Breath. Our town's motto has always been to work with our strengths, and Ameiphus is arguably one of our greatest strengths.

"If we take each batch of Dr. Grenwood's medicine into the Bomb's Breath, we can come out of our coldest, darkest time stronger than we've ever been."

The crowd cheered, a few people whooped, and Aaren smiled at me. It amazed me how much better the town reacted to the suggestion of using the Bomb's Breath now, as opposed to when Mr. Hudson suggested it at the council meeting a few months ago. We'd come a long way.

"We can accomplish great things when we work together. But we can't forget the difference one person can make. Inventing's always been important to us. It's moved our community forward. It's given us the comforts we enjoy. It's made us efficient. It's raised our quality of life." He reached a hand out and placed it on the Difference of One stone. "Every name on this stone is here because their contribution to this community has been great. It's always been our quest to look ahead and look outside what we thought was possible."

I *knew* inventing was important. But this was a celebration! And not even a celebration about inventing, like the Harvest Festival.

"But in trying to look ahead," Mr. Hudson said, "it seems that we sometimes *over*look. It's been our tradition to add names to the Difference of One stone only at the Harvest Festival. However, a onetime change to that tradition was recently put to a secret vote, and everyone chose to add a name to it tonight."

I looked to Aaren and Brock to see if they knew anything about a secret vote, or if they knew of an invention good enough for a special ceremony, but they just grinned.

"Someone in our midst chose to lead a trek to save our town, even though she knew it was extremely dangerous. She didn't let the fear of bandits, the Bomb's Breath, a mountain, or the worst storm this valley's seen since the day she was born stop her."

The words didn't enter my head right. *Is he talking about me?*

"When things got their worst, she didn't back down. When all seemed lost, she faced the bandits' leader alone. By doing so, she saved many lives." He smiled at me. "She saved *my* life. Hope Toriella, I am proud to announce that your name is now engraved in the Difference of One stone." He held out his hand toward me.

A roar erupted from the crowd unlike any I'd heard

before. So many hands patted me on the back as I got to my feet, I practically floated to Mr. Hudson. I turned to the people around the platform. They all looked at me with smiles on their faces. And they clapped and cheered. For me.

They cheered for *me*.

Mr. Hudson pulled a Difference of One medal from his coat pocket, placed it over my head, and gave me a hug. With his head close to my ear, he whispered in a shaky voice, "Thank you."

My mind went to the moment when my invention broke last fall. It had felt like I had a history that was impossible to change—but maybe it *wasn't* so impossible. After all, I never thought I'd live to see my town agree to going anywhere near the Bomb's Breath, yet they cheered for it today.

As a town, we'd changed what would happen next in our history. I guess maybe I had changed what could happen in mine, too.

Acknowledgments

I never realized how hard it would be to write acknowledgments until now. How do you squeeze a million kinds of grateful into so few words? Into *any* words?

First and foremost, I'd like to thank my husband, Lance, and my kids, Kyle, Cory, and Alecia. They have given me everything—their support, their encouragement, their confidence, their tolerance, their love. They never stopped believing in me (or laughing along with me!), even for a second. I'm the luckiest girl in the world to have a family like them. A big thanks to my parents, too, who fostered creativity (no matter how big a mess I made), always listened, and made me believe I could do anything. And to the rest of my family, who have always rallied behind me— especially my sister Kristine Davis, who read some slightly altered passages so many times, I felt like I'd invented a new kind of torture. She deserves a medal.

Huge thanks to Sara Crowe, who somehow manages to emanate a powerful calmness at the same time as a contagious excitement. She is a singularly remarkable agent, and I love working with her.

I couldn't wish for a more amazing editor than Shana Corey. Her incredible ability to focus on the big picture, yet pay attention to the smallest of details and still catch everything in between, is superhuman. She even manages to do it in a way that is kind and keeps me believing in myself and my book. I struck gold when I got her as an editor.

Random House has been a phenomenal publisher—huge thanks to the entire team, especially to Mallory Loehr, the publisher; Nicole de las Heras for her art direction; Alison Kolani, the wonderful copy chief; Adrienne Waintraub for getting my book into school libraries and promoting it at conferences; my publicists, Kathy Dunn and Nicole Banholzer, for their enthusiasm; and sales for all their tireless work.

A massive thanks needs to go to my critique partners. To Erin Summerill, my critique partner/photographer extraordinaire/bestie/go-to girl. She and Rob Code, Jason Manwaring, and David Powers King form my critique group and have been with me from the start and continue to make me a better writer week by week. To Jessie Humphries, who is always willing to drop everything to help me brainstorm or give a critique or lend an ear, and to K. Marie Criddle, who is one of the most amazing people I've ever had the privilege to meet. To my early readers, whose feedback helped immensely: Tammy Merryweather, Cecilia Carter, JaNae Wilson, the Bayles family, the Wheeler family, Taffy Lovell, Nissa Allred, and Miss Wood's fourth-grade class—thank you!

To Brandon Sanderson, who let a newbie writer chat with him at a signing long enough for him to invite her to his class, which changed her life. I'll be forever grateful. And to Joss Whedon, whose commentaries taught me how to tell a story even before I became a writer.

To the 2013 debut authors in the Lucky 13s, for being so helpful, fun, and inspiring.

To my blog readers. You guys rock my world! You've made this journey a million kinds of fun. I love you all!

But most especially, thank you to everyone who reads *Sky Jumpers*. If I could, I'd bake you all cookies.

Don't miss the next Sky Jumpers adventure!

AVAILABLE NOW!

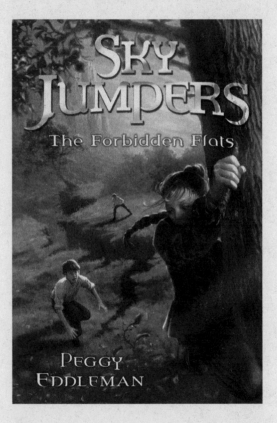

Turn the page for a sneak peek at the first chapter!

The Search

1

I found a foothold on the rough bark of a tree trunk and climbed up in search of Ameiphus. The plants were a lot harder to spot now, since the freezing winter temperatures turned the normally round green leaves as brown and crinkled as the bark they grew on. I swung my leg onto a branch where one was rooted right next to the trunk. The most important part—the whitish mold in the center where all the leaves came together—was still visible. I pulled a flat rock out of my pocket to dig the Ameiphus loose.

Sitting on a branch this high up, on the outside of the mountain crater my town lived in, gave me the best view of the Forbidden Flats. They stretched on as far as I could see. Unlike the last time I saw them—when the bandits attacked four months ago—they were no longer covered in snow. Now they were covered in mud, with tiny grasses and weeds shooting up everywhere. Mr. Allen, my history teacher, said that before the green bombs of World War III, most of this area was farmland that helped to feed an entire nation of people. The weeds and grasses kind of looked like crops—I wondered if springtime back then looked much different.

"Hope!" Brock yelled from the tree next to me as he pushed the dark hair off his forehead. "Staring at the scenery isn't part of our plan!"

I shook myself out of my surroundings-induced stupor and held out the Ameiphus to where it wouldn't hit any branches. Then I dropped it into the bag Aaren clutched down below.

"Got it!" Aaren called. "We're at seventeen!" I could see his grin even from my height.

I spied another Ameiphus plant a little higher, so I climbed up to it. White Rock's council had decided we should find more Ameiphus and process it into the medicine that cured Shadel's Sickness, because people outside our town needed it as much as we did. Not only would it make a valuable trade product, but White Rock would be less of a target if everyone wasn't so desperate for it.

The small forest inside White Rock barely provided enough Ameiphus for our town. But the area outside of our ten-mile-wide crater was covered in forests, too. Dr. Grenwood figured that at least half would get the ideal amount of sunlight for Ameiphus to grow. The best time to harvest was in fall, but she found a way to salvage a lot of the Ameiphus that had been frozen over the winter.

Crews had been coming out here for weeks, gathering what they could. Brock, Aaren, and I went to the council to convince them that we were old enough to leave the protection of our valley and help search. Of course they said no when *I* asked, but luckily for us, adults loved Aaren and he could talk them into anything. Today they let us join the six others who searched the forest floors as we climbed the trees. Our plan was to gather so much Ameiphus that they'd want to send us out here all the time.

Which meant I needed to climb more than gawk. I found a clump of Ameiphus in the crook where almost every branch met the trunk. I dropped it into Aaren's bag and climbed higher. Before long, I was up so high that Aaren looked like a little squirrel, running around to catch the Ameiphus as Brock and I let go of each one.

"I'm going to get more than you!" I shouted to Brock.

"Not a chance," he said, dropping another clump into Aaren's bag.

A bird landed on the branch next to me and cocked his head to the side. I glanced up. I was at least forty feet high already, but the tree went on for a dozen more. I didn't have to worry about climbing high enough that my head would be in the Bomb's Breath, the fifteen-foot-thick band of invisible but deadly air that covered our valley and everywhere else in the world. None of the other people with us were willing to go high enough up the mountain to be anywhere near it, especially since there weren't any warning fences outside our crater. But I wasn't sure if any of the higher branches would hold me.

"I got another." Brock wasn't in sight, but I could hear the smirk in his voice.

Whatever. I could find more than him if I could get down more quickly than I got up. I swung from my branch to get to the one below me.

"Careful!" Aaren's warning reached me right when I realized that my feet couldn't touch the branch below me.

I made the mistake of looking down to see how far I was from the next branch, but I couldn't see it—I only saw my feet, flailing high above the ground. For the first time ever, the height made me dizzy. I held on tightly with one hand and inched the other along the branch toward the trunk. A few of the people who searched close to us must have seen me, because I heard their shouts of concern along with Aaren's and Brock's. I kept reaching out with my foot, trying to catch the trunk, but every time I missed, I swung back and forth and had a harder time holding on. Then everything went quiet. Brock, Aaren, the others— even the birds seemed to hold their breath. I hooked my foot around the trunk, then pulled myself close enough to hug it with my legs. Relief exhaled out of me.

"You okay?" Aaren shouted.

"I think so." I shifted my shaking hands along the branch toward the trunk with more caution than I'd used since we left White Rock two hours earlier. My arms trembled so much, it felt like the entire tree was shaking.

I heard screams from Brock in a tree to my right, along with screams from everyone on the ground. Then I noticed it wasn't actually me that was shaking—it was the tree! The branches swayed as if in a gale-force wind, yet there was no wind at all.

"Hope!" Aaren's terrified voice me made me freeze. I peered down in horror to see what could make my tree move so violently, when I noticed it wasn't only my tree. It was *everything*.

Before long, Brock joined Aaren on the ground, and they both looked as if they couldn't decide whether to run for their lives or stay to save me. I made myself look away from them and focus on moving my hands along until I got to where I could grab hold of the tree trunk. A terrible rumbling echoed off the mountainside, and all our attention jerked to an area one hundred feet to the west, where the earth ripped open as easily as tearing paper. And the crack was traveling in my direction!

I scrambled down the trunk as quickly as I could manage. I grabbed the branches, not even caring that they were ripping up my hands. Getting to the ground fast was all that mattered. My foot slipped and I slid, my cheek scraping the trunk, until I hit a branch.

"You're halfway here!" Aaren yelled. "You can make it!"

I stretched my foot to another branch farther below. Twenty feet more, and I'd be on the ground. Just twenty feet. A loud *crack* sounded all around me and my tree gave a sudden lurch, then swayed, and I knew the split in the ground had reached its roots. The roaring was so loud, I could barely hear anything else. I stayed hugging the trunk with one arm and caught hold of a branch above my head with the other as it began to topple.

Trees cracked and branches broke and people screamed and my heart beat in my ears like the booms that sounded through the depths of the mountain as the tree fell closer and closer to the ground. I tightened my grip and squeezed my eyes shut, but my stomach still knew I was dropping fast.

The tree stopped so suddenly in midair that my legs lost their grip on the trunk and my hands were nearly ripped off the branch. I opened my eyes to see that the trunk had landed against another massive tree that still stood, keeping mine from falling all the way to the ground.

Below me, Brock and Aaren yelled, "Hope, jump!"

I couldn't. A voice inside me screamed *Hang on!* All I could do was clutch the tree with every bit of strength I had.

"Jump! We'll catch you!" I wasn't sure who said it—Brock and Aaren both stood five feet below my legs with their arms outstretched.

Get out of here! a voice inside me pleaded, but I couldn't. Then the *Get out of here!* voice shouted louder than the *Hang on!* voice. I let go and fell.

My body slammed into Aaren and Brock, and we all crashed to the ground. My head was so full of the sounds of the tearing, shaking earth and the need to run that I couldn't tell which body parts hurt. Aaren, Brock, and I struggled to our feet. The ground jerked violently, and I could barely stay upright. We ran, tripped, fell, picked ourselves up, and ran some more, stumble after stumble. Away from the trees crashing to the ground. Away from the earth tearing into pieces. Away from the shaking. Just away.

The earth lurched and we all fell. I tumble-rolled over Brock and down a steep slope, and Aaren landed on top of me at the bottom. I got to my feet, but my legs wouldn't hold me for long before the shaking knocked me back to the ground. Aaren and Brock stood up, their arms out and knees bent and wobbling. We grabbed each other's hands, fearing that one of us would fall away if we let go, and we kept running.

I noticed that two of the six people who were searching for Ameiphus with us were staggering down a hill to the side. I had no idea where the other four were. My lungs burned, but we kept running, trying to escape the crashing trees and splitting earth.

As suddenly as it started, the shaking stopped. Aaren, Brock, and I dropped to the ground, gasping for air. I lay on the forest floor, clutching at weeds, grasses, rocks, and sticks as if they could hold me in place. It felt like the earthquake still shook inside me. I pulled my necklace from under my shirt, held the rough stone pendant from my birth parents, and stroked my thumb and finger down the smooth silver chain from my adoptive parents. Over and over again I rubbed the necklace, as though everything bad would stop if I did.

Before any of us caught our breath enough to speak, I heard shouts in the distance. The other four. Mr. Williams and Stott hobbled toward us with Ben Davies between them, his shirt torn, his arms over their shoulders. Helen Johnson held her arm, which must have been injured. They limped their way to us and collapsed on the ground.

"What was that?" I choked through the dust that coated my throat.

"Earthquake," Stott said.

I shook my head. "An earthquake can't be that bad, can it?"

"They can be that bad." Mr. Williams looked at the mountain where it curved out of sight, toward home. "We need to get back into White Rock. See the damage." He turned to the base of the mountain. "The horses are gone. We'll have to walk."

INVENTION CONTEST

In *Sky Jumpers*, people depend on clever inventions to make their lives easier. Author Peggy Eddleman asked readers to come up with their own inventions. The winning entry is printed in this book! Thank you to everyone who submitted inventions—there were so many great ideas. Visit peggyeddleman.com to see all the entries.

Turn the page to see the winning invention!

CONGRATULATIONS TO THE
WINNER OF THE

SKY JUMPERS

INVENTION CONTEST!

INVENTION: Easy Brush

WHAT IT DOES: Instead of brushing normally, in the handle is an extender, and it goes up and down. So you can just hold the Easy Brush, and it will brush for you.

About the Author

PEGGY EDDLEMAN lives at the foot of the Rocky Mountains in Utah with her husband and their three hilarious and fun kids. *Sky Jumpers* is her first novel.

You can visit Peggy at peggyeddleman.com.